King of the Gunmen

SELECTED FICTION WORKS BY
L. RON HUBBARD

FANTASY
The Case of the Friendly Corpse

Death's Deputy

Fear

The Ghoul

The Indigestible Triton

Slaves of Sleep & The Masters of Sleep

Typewriter in the Sky

The Ultimate Adventure

SCIENCE FICTION
Battlefield Earth

The Conquest of Space

The End Is Not Yet

Final Blackout

The Kilkenny Cats

The Kingslayer

The Mission Earth Dekalogy*

Ole Doc Methuselah

To the Stars

ADVENTURE
The Hell Job series

WESTERN
Buckskin Brigades

Empty Saddles

Guns of Mark Jardine

Hot Lead Payoff

A full list of L. Ron Hubbard's
novellas and short stories is provided at the back.

*Dekalogy—a group of ten volumes

L. RON HUBBARD

King
of the
Gunmen

GALAXY
PRESS

Published by
Galaxy Press, LLC
7051 Hollywood Boulevard, Suite 200
Hollywood, CA 90028

Printed in the United States of America.

ISBN-10 1-59212-402-X
ISBN-13 978-1-59212-402-2

Library of Congress Control Number: 2007903616

Contents

Stories from Pulp Fiction's Golden Age

A ND it *was* a golden age.

The 1930s and 1940s were a vibrant, seminal time for a gigantic audience of eager readers, probably the largest per capita audience of readers in American history. The magazine racks were chock-full of publications with ragged trims, garish cover art, cheap brown pulp paper, low cover prices—and the most excitement you could hold in your hands.

"Pulp" magazines, named for their rough-cut, pulpwood paper, were a vehicle for more amazing tales than Scheherazade could have told in a million and one nights. Set apart from higher-class "slick" magazines, printed on fancy glossy paper with quality artwork and superior production values, the pulps were for the "rest of us," adventure story after adventure story for people who liked to *read*. Pulp fiction authors were no-holds-barred entertainers—real storytellers. They were more interested in a thrilling plot twist, a horrific villain or a white-knuckle adventure than they were in lavish prose or convoluted metaphors.

The sheer volume of tales released during this wondrous golden age remains unmatched in any other period of literary history—hundreds of thousands of published stories in over nine hundred different magazines. Some titles lasted only an issue or two; many magazines succumbed to paper shortages during World War II, while others endured for decades yet. Pulp fiction remains as a treasure trove of stories you can read, stories you can love, stories you can remember. The stories were driven by plot and character, with grand heroes, terrible villains, beautiful damsels (often in distress), diabolical plots, amazing places, breathless romances. The readers wanted to be taken beyond the mundane, to live adventures far removed from their ordinary lives—and the pulps rarely failed to deliver.

In that regard, pulp fiction stands in the tradition of all memorable literature. For as history has shown, good stories are much more than fancy prose. William Shakespeare, Charles Dickens, Jules Verne, Alexandre Dumas—many of the greatest literary figures wrote their fiction for the readers, not simply literary colleagues and academic admirers. And writers for pulp magazines were no exception. These publications reached an audience that dwarfed the circulations of today's short story magazines. Issues of the pulps were scooped up and read by over thirty million avid readers each month.

Because pulp fiction writers were often paid no more than a cent a word, they had to become prolific or starve. They also had to write aggressively. As Richard Kyle, publisher and editor of *Argosy*, the first and most long-lived of the pulps, so pointedly explained: "The pulp magazine writers, the best of them, worked for markets that did not write for critics or attempt to satisfy timid advertisers. Not having to answer to anyone other than their readers, they wrote about human beings on the edges of the unknown, in those new lands the future would explore. They wrote for what we would become, not for what we had already been."

Some of the more lasting names that graced the pulps include H. P. Lovecraft, Edgar Rice Burroughs, Robert E. Howard, Max Brand, Louis L'Amour, Elmore Leonard, Dashiell Hammett, Raymond Chandler, Erle Stanley Gardner, John D. MacDonald, Ray Bradbury, Isaac Asimov, Robert Heinlein—and, of course, L. Ron Hubbard.

In a word, he was among the most prolific and popular writers of the era. He was also the most enduring—hence this series—and certainly among the most legendary. It all began only months after he first tried his hand at fiction, with L. Ron Hubbard tales appearing in *Thrilling Adventures, Argosy, Five-Novels Monthly, Detective Fiction Weekly, Top-Notch, Texas Ranger, War Birds, Western Stories,* even *Romantic Range.* He could write on any subject, in any genre, from jungle explorers to deep-sea divers, from G-men and gangsters, cowboys and flying aces to mountain climbers, hard-boiled detectives and spies. But he really began to shine when he turned his talent to science fiction and fantasy of which he authored nearly fifty novels or novelettes to forever change the shape of those genres.

Following in the tradition of such famed authors as Herman Melville, Mark Twain, Jack London and Ernest Hemingway, Ron Hubbard actually lived adventures that his own characters would have admired—as an ethnologist among primitive tribes, as prospector and engineer in hostile climes, as a captain of vessels on four oceans. He even wrote a series of articles for *Argosy,* called "Hell Job," in which he lived and told of the most dangerous professions a man could put his hand to.

Finally, and just for good measure, he was also an accomplished photographer, artist, filmmaker, musician and educator. But he was first and foremost a *writer,* and that's the L. Ron Hubbard we come to know through the pages of this volume.

This library of Stories from the Golden Age presents the best of L. Ron Hubbard's fiction from the heyday of storytelling, the Golden Age of the pulp magazines. In these eighty volumes, readers are treated to a full banquet of 153 stories, a kaleidoscope of tales representing every imaginable genre: science fiction, fantasy, western, mystery, thriller, horror, even romance—action of all kinds and in all places.

Because the pulps themselves were printed on such inexpensive paper with high acid content, issues were not meant to endure. As the years go by, the original issues of every pulp from *Argosy* through *Zeppelin Stories* continue crumbling into brittle, brown dust. This library preserves the L. Ron Hubbard tales from that era, presented with a distinctive look that brings back the nostalgic flavor of those times.

L. Ron Hubbard's Stories from the Golden Age has something for every taste, every reader. These tales will return you to a time when fiction was good clean entertainment and the most fun a kid could have on a rainy afternoon or the best thing an adult could enjoy after a long day at work.

Pick up a volume, and remember what reading is supposed to be all about. Remember curling up with a *great story*.

—Kevin J. Anderson

KEVIN J. ANDERSON *is the author of more than ninety critically acclaimed works of speculative fiction, including* The Saga of Seven Suns, *the continuation of the Dune Chronicles with Brian Herbert, and his* New York Times *bestselling novelization of L. Ron Hubbard's* Ai! Pedrito!

King of the Gunmen

Chapter One

THE outlook of Kit Gordon was as bleak as the tawny desert which writhed in the heat below his cliff. Never in his thirty-one years had he sunk so far or faced death in such a variety of ways.

And that was saying a great deal, as men had variously dubbed the lean gunslinger "Suicide," "Smoke" and "Sudden Death." From the Missouri to the Pacific, tales were told about the branding fires of the things Kit Gordon was supposed to have done—and sometimes he had done them and always, even if he had not, he was capable of the feats.

Few men could honestly swear that they had met him but his general appearance was very well known. He stood six feet one, hardly thick enough through the waist to cast a shadow were it not for his double guns, swelling out to broad and heavy shoulders which bore up a well-shaped head from which any man, no matter how blind, could have judged his quick intelligence.

His one compelling feature was his eyes. They were changeable with his mood and swiftly so, ranging rapidly from cold killer gray to hot and angry green and even to glowing gold. Men watched his eyes as cattle brokers watch the ticker tape. Their shade was the only thing by which it was possible to predict Kit Gordon's next move.

The men who told stories of him would have been shocked to have seen him now. They stressed the meticulousness of his clothes, the polish of his sixty-dollar boots, the hang of his black broadcloth coat, the set of his expensive John B.

But their description was inaccurate now. Kit's hands were blistering under the onslaught of the savage sun. His coat was white with alkali dust and the Stetson punctured by a rifle bullet. One of his boots had been scuffed beyond repair when his horse had collapsed under him.

His even-featured face was gray with pain and hunger. He was dying and he knew it. But he was not afraid, only annoyed by the circumstances which had led him to such a pass, at his own foolhardy pursuit of Kettle-Belly Plummer and the flight from the lynch mob in the north.

He was still mystified at the rapidity of his downfall, angered by the injustice which had been done.

Two hundred miles north, at the Santa Fe whistling post of Randall, his hotel room had been looted in his absence and his change of clothing had vanished. A private inquiry had elicited the information that the gunman named Plummer, an enemy of old standing, had been seen in the vicinity. Kit Gordon had preferred to do his own justice, had taken the trail.

But he had found no trace of Kettle-Belly Plummer though he had searched for two days in the surrounding country. He would not have cared about the suit and hat and boots. But among the loot had been a repeater watch, a favored possession and good-luck piece worth around a thousand dollars. That watch had once been the property of Kettle-Belly Plummer until that unworthy had lost it across the faro table in Dodge, two years before. In the following fight, Kit Gordon had kept the watch.

Trying to think of some way to get a line on the obvious thief, Kit had returned to Randall, intending to press his inquiry even further. His reception was amazing.

The town marshal, backed by a mob of railroad workers, had tried to arrest him and Kit, knowing a lynch mob when he saw one, had resisted. Before the marshal and two section hands had thumped into the dust of the street, Kit Gordon had been hit and hit hard with a bullet in his right shoulder but he had managed to escape.

The only intelligence he had of the affair was that he had been *seen* leading the gang which had stopped and robbed the Limited the night before, dynamiting the express car and killing a messenger.

Kit knew the answer to that. Plummer was settling the score in his own back-knifing way. If Kit could only find Plummer . . .

His tongue swelling in his mouth from thirst, with hanging behind him and torturous death at hand, he lay exhausted, watching the maddening mirages come and go, growing palm trees and spouting fountains from the caustic sand. A train puffed importantly where a train would never run. A town fried a hundred feet in the air.

The town was what interested Kit. It was certainly somewhere near at hand or else it could not have its picture projected upon the shimmering sky in that ridiculous fashion.

His head felt light and through it ran the crazy string of his thoughts. He considered the town with a practiced eye, even amused when it occurred to him that he was inspecting something which was probably a hundred miles away and far beyond the normal range of sight.

He could read the signs very clearly. The Bird Cage Opera House. The *Seco Hombre* Saloon. Wells Fargo's stage was drawn up before the post office and the citizens were standing about.

As is the trick of the mirage at times, all things were greatly magnified so that the men and horses appeared ten times their usual size.

One fellow in particular attracted Kit Gordon's attention. The man was very tall and thickly built, with a black beard and a black hat. He hovered on the rim of the crowd as though he did not want to be seen and then, abruptly, turned on his heel and sprinted for a horse.

With one foot in the stirrup, he started to mount. The men in the crowd seemed to be very agitated as they started toward him on the run.

And then, as is the habit of the mirage, having started the drama it refused to longer amuse Kit Gordon by completing it. Empty air writhed with heat waves and the town was gone.

Palm trees came again to wave in false breezes. A waterfall poured endless tons of water down in clouds of cool spray. And then palms and waterfall also vanished.

A lake which spread for endless leagues appeared to sparkle, cool and inviting, before Kit's tortured gaze.

He shut his eyes. Soon enough he would go mad and

start to run toward those things. No use to devil himself by watching now. Maybe he had been wrong in running away. Death at the end of the rope and dancing lightly upon the air would have been much preferable to dying thus, by slow torture, wounded, starved and alone. His two Colts did him no good now. They would not command a desert's heat or bully the stones into giving drink.

Even if someone happened to find him, his moment of life would only be lengthened long enough to get him into shape for a hanging so that he would make a presentable corpse.

Painfully he crawled into the comparative shade of a boulder and pillowed his head upon his arm.

He was again in the sun when he suddenly came to life. He sat up, listening. A drumming of hoofs was a throb in the earth more than a sound in the air. Even now, half dead, the instinct for battle was rising strongly within his wasted being.

To his left was the deep gash of a pass, evidently the only way through and up to this lava rimrock. But the sounds were not from there.

He swept the desert's blaze with his tortured sight and though motes of sunlight danced like a curtain, he made out the dots of running horses in the distance underneath a great pall of yellow dust.

Restively he sought for the energy required to move and finally dragged it from the almost exhausted well of strength. He took a Colt in his left hand and inched closer to the rim. It was barely possible that the posse from the north had trailed him all that way.

But no, these men were coming from the south. One was

in the lead, three hundred yards in front of a compact mass of horsemen.

Their approach was very swift and as the lead man neared, a puff of dust leaped before him and a shot sounded from the men behind. The lone rider was evidently striving to make this break in the blank face of the stretching buttes even as Kit had made it too many hours ago to think about it.

The man was close enough to give Kit a general idea of his appearance. He was huge and thickly built, wearing a black Stetson and a blacker beard.

It seemed to Kit's privation-distorted memory that he had known this big fellow once. Somehow he confused himself with the man's flight, the posse below with the posse which had trailed Kit.

He was stripped down to his fundamental self, was Kit, and it was his second nature which compressed the trigger of the Colt.

The kick of it made his whole body ache. Through the shredding smoke of the shot he saw a man flop off his mount and vanish under the hoofs of fellow riders.

The black-bearded one in the lead glanced up that hundred-foot wall of lava with a startled shout.

Kit fired into the running horsemen again and once more his bullet took toll. He did not have to see to shoot or even consciously try. It would have been more difficult to have missed than to have hit. Such was the reputation of Kit Gordon. And even now, footfalls already echoing along the golden pavement of the Devil's corridors of black, he could squeeze his trigger and count on his man with a Colt at seventy-five yards and more.

The black-bearded one vanished into the defile. The horsemen out front were a tangled mass of horses trying to turn and getting run down.

The Colt fired with methodical, terrifying precision. Three men were lumps upon the hot sand when the horsemen finally fled out of range. Nor did the posse pause for an instant for even a backward glance. They were hidden by their own mask of dust and when it had settled they were nothing but hoofmarks on the desert floor.

Kit turned around and looked toward the pass. The shooting had cleared his head and now he was wondering a little if he had had any business taking part in the unexpected drama.

The man with the black beard came with admirable caution. He put his hat up on the end of a mesquite stick and waited for several minutes. When nothing happened he exposed a cautious eye. Kit did not look very formidable at the moment. The man took heart and advanced with a lumbering stride.

He stood looking down at Kit for some time as though his eyesight could plumb Kit's head and read the reasons for that sudden and welcome aid.

Kit managed a grin and though the effect was ghastly, the stranger knew the smile was well meant.

"I know where I saw you," said Kit, speaking slowly and trying to keep his tongue from clogging his speech. "You were walking around a hundred feet in the air. That's it. A hundred feet in the air."

The Colt fired with methodical, terrifying precision.
Three men were lumps upon the hot sand when
the horsemen finally fled out of range.

The look on the stranger's face was intended to be consoling. "That's all right, friend. You just take it easy. I got some water on my horse."

Kit nodded, showing a gentlemanly willingness to accept a small favor like that. He grinned anew. "You were walking around back of a stagecoach in front of the post office and suddenly you decided to light out hell for leather. You grabbed a horse at the hitch rack, and the stagecoach and the crowd and the horse were all a hundred feet in the air. That's where I met you."

The stranger was clearly astounded. He cocked his big shaggy head on one side and his blue eyes were wide open with wonder.

"You mentioned water?" said Kit, trying not to be eager. But even that thought could not be sustained in his thirst-dazed mind. He had seen something bright on the stranger's vest. An oval badge. . . .

"You're a sheriff!" said Kit, drawing back, half-minded to snatch for his Colt. But the other man did not seem to find anything odd in being a sheriff or in Kit.

"Sure, pardner. I'm Rainbow Jackson, sheriff of Yancy County, Arizona. And if you're going to speak derogatory of my recent flight from the irate citizens of Gunsmoke, you can be plenty certain it was a *dernier resort. Honi soit qui mal y pense,* says I. That's French. I ain't cussin'. It means a guy that'd think it wasn't right ought to be booted in the pants. When sheepherders get up nerve enough to pack guns and shoot and when they don't show no predilection for peace, I prefers to use speed and horse sense in my own peculiar way. What ain't going to be done *vi et armis* has got to be done with brains—and I ain't got no army to speak of at the moment. . . ."

Rainbow Jackson's voice seemed to come from a long distance and the visibility was growing dense before Kit's face. "You said something about water?" He was still trying to appear as a gentleman should.

Chapter Two

DURING the days which followed, Kit Gordon was but faintly aware of his surroundings. He was never at any time delirious, but he had gone so long on nerve alone that he had a long ways to build before he could begin to think clearly.

One evening the flash of reason did not immediately depart. For some time he lay quietly in the blankets wondering when he would blink out again. But this time he did not. His shoulder ached but not seriously. His head, for a change, felt cool. He was possessed of a physique too splendid to be so easily vanquished.

Experimentally he turned over. They were camped beside a hidden water hole in the mountains and all about them towered black cliffs. They were evidently safe enough for the moment—at least from the citizens of Gunsmoke.

Rainbow Jackson was making some coffee over a low, smokeless fire, humming gently to himself about a lady named Susannah. He sensed that Kit was awake and turned on his heels to look at him.

"Hello, pardner. How do you feel?"

"Fine," said Kit. "How long have I been out?"

"About five days. But, hell, I wasn't goin' noplace anyhow. Kettle-Belly Plummer and his ba-bas has got themselves a *cordon sanitaire* all around these hills, just hopin' I ain't got sense enough to stay hid. And I got a hunch that includes you too."

Kit lay very quietly. "Plummer?"

"Yeah, Kettle-Belly Plummer. You ought to have heard of him someplace. He's so proddy he'd shoot his horse for gruntin' back. He's tough as a horned toad and if he bit a sidewinder, the snake'd die for shore. He says, with plenty reason, that there ain't one man in Arizony that'd dare stand up to him in an even break. Nobody knows about that on account of nobody, so far, has had either the chance nor the nerve, most of Kettle-Belly's victims dyin' of lead poisonin' from behind. They say there's only one lead-slinger that'd stand up to him and that's a gent named Suicide Gordon."

"You . . . you've met this Gordon?" said Kit.

"Me? Hell, no. I'm not countin' on meetin' him, either, no more'n I am Kettle-Belly. I'm a *terrae filius,* a son of the earth, and I don't go hobnobbin' around with gods and devils so careless as all that. I'm shakin' in my ample boots at the thought of meetin' this Kettle-Belly face to face. I'm plumb tenacious when it comes to wantin' to keep on livin'."

Jackson poured out a cup of steaming coffee and handed it to Kit, following it with a cigarette he had rolled for him as he talked.

"Kind of funny," said Jackson, sitting back on his spurs like some gigantic bear, "me havin' warrants for Kettle-Belly and his pals and them chasin' me like hounds hole a rabbit."

He fished into his many big pockets. He seemed to be padded with papers and it took him some time to find the warrants for which he searched. Out of his personal file cases fell a square reward poster which fluttered to earth within reach of Kit's hand. He could read it without touching it.

Five Thousand Dollars Reward. $5000
Will be paid by the
Sante Fe Railroad
For KIT GORDON
Dead or Alive.

Gordon is six feet one, brown hair, gray eyes. Last seen was wearing black coat, white Stetson, and was wounded in right shoulder. He is desperate and equally good with either left hand or right. He is wanted for the murder of a Sante Fe engineer and other crimes.

Kit tried not to appear uneasy. Jackson was still looking for the warrants and finally located them. He showed them to Kit.

"Y'see," said Jackson, "the cattlemen in these parts went and elected me to office. And then sheep began to be shipped in here and I had to do something to keep peace, so I tried to stop the sheep rather than have a war. That put me on the outs with the ba-bas. But what I didn't know was that wool was going to soar like it did and all of a sudden the whole blamed range began to turn white with the woollies. The cattlemen pitched in and began to shoot sheep and then the big sheep combine got into action and imported a bunch of fancy gunhawks and Apaches, and things have begun to commence. Kettle-Belly is their general in the field and the cattlemen are diving for their holes.

Out of his personal file cases fell a square reward poster which fluttered to earth within reach of Kit's hand.

"Last week I still had a chance to do something, so I issued orders that nobody was to wear guns in Gunsmoke and swore out these warrants to make Kettle-Belly quit his shootin' spree. Along comes a shipment of Henry rifles and Winchesters on that stage and I was fool enough to open my mouth about it. The crowd gets peeved and I has to light out. They know I'm all for the cattle interests and as long as I'm alive, I got plenty of evidence against this sheep combine for all these killin's. And now you got dragged into this mess and tallied three notches, and I hate to have to tell you that the country has stopped bein' healthy for either of us."

"Aren't you going to do something?" said Kit.

"Me? I'm a timid man, pardner."

Kit knew that this was modesty despite the sheriff's actions. "Do you have any plans?"

Jackson scratched and stroked his beard. "Well . . . yes. I sent word to the Arizony Rangers and I think maybe I'll sashay around and get together these demoralized punchers and clean up Yancy County. Steele's Ranch is the headquarters for the cattlemen and as soon as you can travel, we'll head for there. We got to have law and respect for the statutes in this here country. *Sic semper tyrannis,* says I. The day of the gunman has gone with the buffaler."

"And you're counting me in on this?" said Kit.

"Not unless you want to be counted in. When Kettle-Belly Plummer is around I don't blame nobody for walkin' light. Y'ever meet him?"

Kit shut his eyes and the scene of two years back leaped into action beneath the lids. It was a street in Dodge and

Kettle-Belly Plummer was swaggering down the high boardwalk.

"There ain't room for two gunslingers in this trail town," he heard Plummer saying. "Either you light out or I'll see that you do, Gordon."

Plummer, king bully, had not taken kindly to Kit Gordon's quiet statement that he, Plummer, was all wind and no smoke.

Guns flashed and Plummer dropped to his knees. But the man was not dead, only shot through the thigh. . . .

Kit looked at Rainbow Jackson. "I've seen him, yes."

"Then I don't blame you for walkin' light, pardner. I'll give you grub and I caught some of these horses you dismounted and you can beat it with my heartiest regrets and earnest thanks for what you done."

The reward poster was fluttering in the evening wind, just a few feet from Kit's hand. Light out? But where would he go? He had no money and it was the sheerest luck that he was not known in this particular region.

"No. I'll stick it," said Kit.

"Good boy. What'd you say your name was?"

"Mason," said Kit.

"Mason," repeated the sheriff thoughtfully as he gathered up the papers including the reward poster and stuffed them into his pockets. "Funny I never heard of you. You dropped three men, plugged 'em as neat as could be. You're a left-hander, too."

"Sure," said Kit. "I'm a left-hander."

"Y'know," said Jackson, "I'm fairly timid. But the law of Judge Colt is over. Such guys as Masterson and Gordon and Plummer has outlived their day. We got to have law by the

18

book and I'm dead agin' all this slaughter. *Lex talionis* has got to stop and *lex scripta* must triumph. That's the eye-for-an-eye business and the code of the books," he added helpfully.

"Yes," replied Kit, sipping his coffee. "But these men have developed their art out of necessity. Maybe they aren't any worse at heart than Wild Bill Hickok—excluding Plummer, of course, due to his record of ambush kills. They aren't all *ambuscaderos*. Now take Gordon, for instance. Supposing he was on your side."

"Gordon!" said Jackson violently. "On *my* side! He's never been on the side of the law and he'll never turn."

"But supposing he had and you met him. What would you do?"

Jackson didn't need to think about it. "I wouldn't give him a chance. He doesn't rate one. To hell with his reputation for even breaks. I'd take him any way I could and rid the West of a man-killer."

"And collect the reward?" said Kit, gently.

"Reward? To hell with a reward. I'm on the side of the law and I know what's right and what's wrong. Suicide Gordon is wanted for murder up north and that's enough. In spite of last week's fiasco, sometimes I get on my hind laigs and snort, and if I was to meet Gordon I'd send him north in a rush with enough iron on him to break his back. I got too many killers in Yancy County already and before I'm through, there won't be one. *Lex scripta* is king and be damned to your gunslingers!"

He realized then, did Jackson, that he had been speaking with great heat. He grinned apologetically through his beard. "Aw, I ain't as tough as all that. But I do say that the day of the killer is done and as far as I'm concerned this guy Gordon doesn't rate an even break from the law. I don't care what the circumstances was, I'd stay behind my badge and hand him over. I got some honor left. But the devil with that. Soon as you think you can travel, we'll get over to Steele's Ranch and see what Arizony is going to do to help us out. And as for you, Mason, I'm glad to have you takin' an interest in our war. I'll deputize you—"

"No thanks," said Kit hurriedly.

"Have it your own way, pardner," replied Jackson. "*Humanum est errare,* says I, meanin' a man can't help but make mistakes."

Chapter Three

THREE days later, when Rainbow Jackson thought the *"cordon sanitaire"* had withdrawn from the picketing of a few thousand rugged acres of buttes and when Kit Gordon was barely able to travel, they headed out for the Steele Ranch.

All day they rode as Indians ride: stopping at every rise and bellying up to search the fields ahead for signs of the enemy, examining every trampled patch of sand, dismounting to scrutinize afoot the most likely ambush spots.

Kit had changed clothes with a less messily killed rider and aside from the hole in the checkered shirt just above the heart and the black stains upon the batwings, the costume became him well. His pain-drawn face was transformed by suffering of the past many days and, at a swift glance, he was not much different from the multitude—unless one happened to merit the full impact of his eyes.

"Say," said Rainbow Jackson as they dismounted to examine a water hole for tracks, "you seem to be as interested in this thing as me."

"The excitement, I guess," said Kit. "And what man wouldn't be interested in preserving his own life? If there are as many sheepherders packing guns in Yancy County as you say there is, then ten times this much caution would be too little. A long time ago the thought of getting plugged between the shoulder blades by a man you've never met lost its romantic attraction for me."

"Sure. But are you pos'tive this meeting between you and Kettle-Belly Plummer was *casual*?"

"Very casual," said Kit.

Rainbow did not appear to be very convinced but he mounted and they continued in silence.

Kit was too busy figuring out the hand he held to pay much attention to his companion's mood. The outrage which he had first felt because of Plummer was simmering down to a cold and deadly brew, something more bitter than hatred and needing only the seasoning of powder smoke to bring it to his taste. Thoughtfully he calculated on the portion of Plummer's anatomy which could be best drilled without bringing any possible harm to that beloved repeater watch. This time it wouldn't be a warning shot in the thigh. This time . . .

They had come out of the hills and were winding down a heat-scorched trail about two feet wide when they heard the far-off firing.

Rainbow shot a comprehensive glance back at Kit. "Hear that, Mason? Looks like Plummer and his friends has got there first!"

He put an exclamation point to it with a crack of his quirt. Recklessly he spurred his horse down the trail at a run. Kit followed and when they reached the sodded plain, he ranged up beside Jackson and then, because of the other's weight, began to surge ahead.

"Hold on there!" shouted Rainbow into the gale of his own creation. "You can't go bustin' into that mess! Wait for me!"

But Kit was not waiting. The plain sped by beneath his mount's flying hoofs and as he rode he unlimbered his left Colt. His right arm was still in a sling but he used the hand to hold the reins.

The way was long and the goal was not yet in sight when the firing began to sputter out. From time to time it revived in a furious burst and then subsided to drop even lower than before.

Ahead was a small ridge and beyond that lay the Steele Ranch, in a cuplike depression. Kit streaked up the slope and hauled in to a rearing halt just under the crest. He was off, and running, before his horse was solidly back to earth.

Kit lunged into a lying posture, taking cover behind a big black stone. With one swift rake he took in the entire situation below.

The ranch houses were already burning, fired by an Apache arrow trick. The bodies of several horses dotted the corral. Other black lumps marked the places where men had died, guns in hand.

From the last house to burn, three punchers rushed, terror quickening their strides, batwings flapping grotesquely. They were headed toward the corral until they saw that all the horses were dead. They spun about, striving to make the cover of a hayrick.

A shattering blast of gunfire sprayed them. Two dropped and lay still. The third stumbled, fell on his face, striving to hitch himself forward with his hands and arms, eyes bent agonizingly upon the safety just ahead.

From the cover of the opposite rim from Kit's, a tall

black-garbed man stood up, rifle carelessly held. The distance was two hundred yards, but Kit had the eyes of memory with which to see that man. He was bulging but hard as a bullet. His big face was an unhealthy white. His eyes were black pinpoints almost lost in the folds of his big jowls.

It was Kettle-Belly Plummer.

He lifted the rifle to his shoulder and took casual aim at the wounded puncher below.

The range was too great for a Colt. Kit had hoped for a better chance than this, but though his reputation was that of a killer, he could not remain quiet as witness to the murder of a wounded man.

It was no use to aim. He sent a slug yowling away from the rocks twenty feet to Plummer's left, the place where it would make the most vicious sound.

Plummer vanished from sight.

Kit turned to see Rainbow inching up, shoving a rifle through the grass ahead of him. The muzzle was quite close. Kit snatched it to him, levered a cartridge into the chamber and waited tensely for Plummer to again show himself.

The outlaw did not show any particular fondness for exchanging lead with a man he could not see and whose identity he could not guess. The entire rim remained blank except for one fluttering patch where the wind rippled the dirty shirt of a sheepherder who hung, arms dangling, from the cover he had thought safe.

Minutes dragged and still nothing stirred.

Restlessly, Jackson crept around the edge of the rim, trying to discover the whereabouts of the gang. Presently dust began to fan up from the ridges beyond and Jackson crawled back to Kit.

"They beat it," said Rainbow.

"Damn!" spat Kit.

"You seem to be pretty mad about it."

"Yeah. Any man that'd shoot a wounded puncher ought to be shot himself."

The smoke from the rancho buildings was growing thicker, to hang like a shroud over the small valley. The first flames had eagerly lapped into the dry timber but now their food was less easy to assimilate.

"They probably thought we was fifty," said Rainbow. "They wasn't takin' no chances of gettin' outflanked. *Dieu défend le droit,* says I. Let's go down."

They walked through the gathering smoke toward the place the last men had been shot, being careful to sing out as they went to prevent any possible sniping.

The wounded man lay exhausted behind the rick, panting, face down in the yellow hay, hands as stiff as talons. Kit turned him over and saw that the bullet had passed through the boy's abdomen. There could be no saving him.

"Steele's boy," said Rainbow, softly. "Anything I can do, Eddy?"

The younger Steele unclenched his eyes and stared at Jackson. It took him some time to win the fight for control of his voice. "Hello . . . Sheriff. Looks like they wiped us out. . . . You should have got here . . . sooner."

"This gent's the only one that's with me," said Rainbow. "Where's your pa?"

Eddy Steele struggled to suppress the hoarseness of his breathing. "We run the damned ba-bas off . . . last month. They got dad alive, without him ever knowin' what happened . . . and took him God knows where. There was four of us in the house but . . . they burned us out. You'll . . . you'll get them, Rainbow?"

"Sure, son."

"Two of you . . . ain't enough. There must have been fifty up there . . . I think . . . I . . ."

Kit felt the stiffening of the youngster's shoulders. The eyes abruptly focused upon the far distance and glazed. Kit eased the body to the earth.

There was nothing they could do at the ranch but they had no place to go. They salvaged a few supplies from the partially demolished cook shack and cooked a dismal supper by raking coals away from the collapsed house.

Midnight found them sleepless.

For hours Kit Gordon had not spoken. But now, seeing that Rainbow was not asleep, he addressed him abruptly. "How long has this Plummer been down here?"

"Two weeks, three weeks."

"Yeah," said Kit.

They were silent for some time and then a rustling sound beyond the smoldering coals of the barn brought them to their feet, hands gripping the cold butts of their guns.

By the eerie red light they saw a small man in white leading his horse aimlessly and wonderingly across the clearing.

"Lookin' for somebody?" said Rainbow.

The fellow gave a start and stopped, peering into the shadows.

"Are you Mr. Steele?" he said.

"Steele's dead," said Rainbow.

The fellow appeared to be very undecided but he was obviously alone. Kit and Rainbow walked out toward him.

"I'm Judge Carruthers," said the stranger. "I was supposed to meet Mr. Steele and some of the cattlemen here concerning a matter of grave importance."

"*Grave* importance is right," said Rainbow grimly. "Where the hell are the Rangers?"

Judge Carruthers peered through the red dimness at Rainbow and then gave a relieved sigh of recognition. "You're Jackson, the sheriff of Yancy County. I'm glad to meet you, sir."

Rainbow took the hand and shook it and dropped it. "And now I repeat. Where's the Rangers?"

"I am sorry," said the judge. "There must be some misunderstanding. I thought this was a matter of having no official court to arbitrate the differences which we understood to exist between certain sheep interests and some small cattlemen here."

"You mean the sheep interests has got something to say in Prescott," said Rainbow. "*Revenons à nos moutons,* says the governor."

"Ah, yes," said Judge Carruthers, "let us return to our sheep!"

"Yeah," said Rainbow. "And to hell with the bovines. How much money did the sheep combine pay to the state to hold off the Rangers?"

"Sir! I cannot allow you to impute—"

"The devil with that. Do you know what's happening in Yancy County? A gang of cutthroats has moved in and any man that ever had anything to do with cattle is being murdered! Impute and be damned! Why the hell did you come down here? What in God's name could *you* do?"

"Sir," said the judge, "I am here to hear the grievances and dispense justice. It is my intention to call a court together in Gunsmoke and make an end to these hostilities. Rangers would only complicate matters."

Rainbow looked thoughtfully at the judge. The man was not very impressive. He was wearing a white suit and an ascot tie with gold stickpin and flowing collar. He had a perpetually startled pair of white eyebrows and a face red with overeating, matched by a colored nose.

Rainbow rubbed his beard and scowled. "Well . . ." he said hesitantly, "I been preachin' that nothin' good would ever come of arms and that the law books has got to triumph. *Lex scripta* forever above *lex talionis,* says I. There's been enough scrappin' already. You mean that, Judge?"

"I have full powers and I accept your apologies."

"I didn't offer none," grinned Rainbow, easier now that he had made up his mind. "But if you can bring an end to this war, that's what we all want. You can get them to divide the range and quit this killin'. Okay, Judge, we'll burn trail for Gunsmoke. Come on, Mason."

Kit Gordon shook his head slowly. "I didn't take that badge, if you remember. Besides, I have a few affairs of my own."

Rainbow shrugged. "Well, if you won't, you won't. But damn it, Mason, you hadn't ought to run out on me this way. I was plannin' on keepin' you around for a spell."

The implied position of superiority was not meant that way and Kit overlooked it. "If you'll take my advice, Rainbow, keep wide of Gunsmoke."

"Aw, hell, them gents can't overlook the law the way they been doin'. This country is gettin' civilized."

Kit looked around at the smoldering ruins. "Sure. I wish you luck with your court, Rainbow."

"Be seein' you, Mason."

Chapter Four

GUNSMOKE straggled toward the Silver Palace Saloon. Most of the sheepmen had come in from the range to see that "justice" would be done, and had made a considerable spree of the affair the night before.

The clean-faced puncher and his batwings seemed to have vanished from the dusty desert town and the species of horse which was ranged along on both sides of the street appeared quite different from that recently tied to the hitch racks. In reality, the horses were the same, as they had been rounded up from the ravaged ranches. But no currycombs had striven to take the burs from their tails and no oats had been meted out to make them happy, and so they stood in suffering dejection, hardly batting an ear at the uproar which clamored all about them.

Yancy County had indeed taken a turn for the worse. Sheepherders, to a cattleman's way of thinking, were bad enough. But these men were several steps lower upon the social rung. They had been culled from the sweeping backwash of the railroad gangs, from the jails of the Mississippi Valley. To the number of three hundred they had slouched in to take up their duties as none-too-gentle shepherds.

They smelled of sheep and followed like sheep and the combined babble of their voices was a mimicry of their charges.

These men had no need of high heels or spurs or chaps. Their jeans were as dirty and ragged as their shirts. And, often as not, they wore small Eastern hats and caps.

To Kit Gordon they were especially disgusting as they had brought something mean and sordid to a land which had been clean as a crystal goblet. Such rabble had followed the pioneers along the Mississippi, the Forty-Niners, the striving frontiersmen. Yancy County had been wrested from Mexican and Apache at the cost of clean western blood.

Certainly that awful payment in lives and suffering had not bought Arizona for this.

Kit was squatting on his heels in the shade of the general store, watching the Silver Palace Saloon gulp the mob. His face had not felt a razor for many weeks which gave him an effective disguise. Few men could recall seeing Suicide Gordon unshaven and unwashed. It was a new and thoroughly distasteful experience. His skin crawled under the coarse, dirty touch of his cotton shirt. His legs were uncomfortable in the rough new jeans—denim too new to be soft and still shedding its bluish tint at the contact of a sweaty thigh.

He had cached his spurs and gunbelts and sling. The Colts were hard and uncomfortable inside the waistband of his pants and though this would slow down his draw, the holsters had been too ornate, too well known.

For two hot hours he had watched for Plummer without result. Evidently the outlaw was already inside the Silver Palace having entered from the back, taking no chances with any stray rifle shot. That was what made Kettle-Belly Plummer so dangerous—he took no chances of any kind and was always certain to snatch up and use any slight advantage or sportsmanship against, and of, an enemy.

Kit knew the man. And the very fact that he had once bested Plummer in an even break now reduced his chances at repeating such a scene.

With the town swarming with Plummer's verminous kind, Kit knew too well how dangerous was his present position. He had already seen a dozen men he knew at sight. Not one of the dozen would fail to think about that five-thousand-dollar reward in the instant he saw Kit Gordon.

Judge Carruthers and Rainbow Jackson came down the street toward the Silver Palace, looking like a hobgoblin and a grizzly keeping company. Rainbow was watchful and nervous, his big paws hovering constantly near his Colt. Rainbow knew that he walked on the edge of his grave but Kit Gordon could almost hear him muttering, *"Lex scripta* over *lex talionis."*

It was a fine theory, this law by the book as opposed to law by might, but Gunsmoke, that hot afternoon, did not appear to be the most favorable place in the world to demonstrate it.

Rainbow was thoroughly identified with the cattlemen of the region—too thoroughly. And though not one puncher could be seen the entire length of this fast-emptying street, Rainbow was carrying on. Kit could not but admire such strength of conviction in the face of past events.

The blow as struck by Plummer against the cattle interests had been swift and paralyzing. The small outfits of the country had not been warned in time, had been unable to effect a mobilization, had found themselves without funds or arms. Not more than eighty punchers in all were scattered through

Yancy County after the death toll of the past weeks. And the eighty, no matter how brave, were nothing against this well-armed, carefully organized rabble.

The last man had entered the saloon. Casually, Kit stood up and strolled through the dust toward the Silver Palace. The place babbled with many voices but as he reached the top of the steps, a sharp rap as of a six-gun on mahogany quieted the crowd.

Kit eased through the door and stood with his back to the wall, looking over the heads of the mob at the back bar. The place was alive with odor and the contact with sheep was more than strong. It was hot and stale and less strong stomachs would have objected violently.

Rainbow was standing at the end of the bar. "Order in the court. Stand up while the judge takes his seat!"

The saloon, its gaming tables thrust back against the walls, was very capacious, containing the two hundred and fifty sheepmen with ease. All the two hundred and fifty kept their seats, exchanging grins, leaning back in their chairs and benches and lighting up cigarettes and pipes to thicken the already carvable atmosphere.

Big Rainbow Jackson glowered and his beard bristled as he broadsided them with his displeasure. This occasioned a mutter of mirth in the audience and Rainbow brought down his six-gun butt hard enough to crack the mahogany.

"Shut up, you fuzz-tails!" he bellowed. "You might think you own Yancy County, but by God, this is a court of the State of Arizony and you'll act like human bein's or else!"

The mirth was no longer suppressed and Kit could see a

dull crimson glow overspread the sheriff's face and vanish beneath the beard.

The din took some time to echo from wall to bare clapboard wall and then it quieted—but only because those assembled wanted to enjoy the show to its fullest power to amuse.

Judge Carruthers came out of one of the gambling rooms at the rear and walked as judicially as possible to a chair which had been set on packing cases at the end of the bar.

Inadvisedly, Carruthers had donned a black gown the better to lend dignity to his office. His round body did little to fill it out and a train brushed up the dust in his tracks.

From one end of the West to the other almost every man in the room had had sufficient cause to shudder a little at this display of legality. From habit they were still; but only for an instant. A gale of guffaws which made the weather-beaten shack rock upon its flimsy foundations almost knocked Carruthers from his feet. He stopped in trepidation, his perpetually raised brows shooting even higher, his jaw slackening. He shut his mouth the better to swallow. That sea of amused humanity would have unnerved a braver man than the judge and all hint of pomposity had vanished from his mien when he again approached the chair which, in itself, was a burlesque.

The crowd quieted as though awaiting the next gag and then their reward was certain. The chair had not been securely anchored, and heavy, round Carruthers was only saved by Rainbow's quick snatch at its back.

Angrily, drowned in laughter, Rainbow kicked the packing cases out of the way and set the chair down on the floor. Like a whipped dog, Carruthers sidled into it, casting frightened glances at his "courtroom."

The fog of smoke mingled with the stench of sheep grew heavier, making it difficult for Kit to see the back bar clearly. Evidently some of the audience were also having visibility troubles and three men opened the windows by the simple expedient of throwing empty bottles through them. More than anything else, this bore home to Carruthers that he was dealing with an ungovernable rabble.

Kit was thoroughly disgusted but he was helpless. Any move on his part to assert himself would have brought an untimely death in its immediate wake. He had to stand at the back of the room and watch Rainbow suffer, much as he wanted to help him.

Carruthers put a timid inquiry to the sheriff and Rainbow stood back to roar, "Where's the lawyer for the cattle interests?"

Another laugh had not yet gotten started when Plummer made his appearance through a side door, swaggering toward the bar. Kit remarked to himself that Kettle-Belly Plummer was putting on weight. The face was more puffy than ever, the eyes further withdrawn and seemingly smaller. The room was still and awed.

Plummer fixed Carruthers with a leer. "He couldn't come, friend."

Rainbow stuck out his jaw. "Y'mean you ran him out of town so he couldn't appear. Y'tryin' to obstruct the course of justice! I'm warnin' you, Plummer, you're through gettin' your way because you've got a pack of ba-bas at your back. This is a court of the State of Arizony. The day's gone when gunmen can do any damn thing they think up. *Lex scripta,* pardner, has come to stay and *lex talionis* has been shoved out the rear door."

Plummer looked menacingly at Jackson, his big hand swinging near the butt of his well-worn, many-notched .45. He spoke in a hard voice.

"Cut the fancy talk, Jackson. Don't git fancy around here just because you got marooned in the mountains one winter with a dictionary to read." This brought a landslide of cheers from the audience. "What are you talkin' about?" resumed Plummer, after acknowledging the applause.

"*Lex scripta* is what you get in the law books and *lex talionis* is Latin fer the law of the talons. Now do you savvy, you ignorant he-goat?"

Rainbow's remarks were not well received by either the crowd or Plummer. However, Plummer was having his day, as every canine must, and he felt magnanimous.

"Let," said Plummer, "the trial go on."

"This isn't a trial," ventured Carruthers after clearing his throat. "I was to arbitrate between the cattle and sheep interests of this county. . . ."

"You're a judge, ain't you?" challenged Plummer.

"Why . . . yes . . . I . . ."

"Okay," said Plummer. "We got a trial for you."

Jackson shoved his bulk half over the bar and glared at Plummer. "You don't seem to savvy plain English, to say nothin' of educated Latin. I'm sheriff in this county and by God, when there's trials to be had, I'll do the arresting and specifyin'. I tell you, the strong-arm stuff won't go. Arizony is gettin' civilized and gents like you and Masterson and Ben Thompson and Doc Holliday and Suicide Gordon is over. All over! The judge is goin' to arbitrate an'—"

"Bring in the prisoners!" called Plummer toward the door, deliberately turning his back upon Rainbow.

The judge cast a despairing glance at Jackson and then sighed as he looked toward the door. The sigh had been one of complete resignation to his fate.

Chapter Five

UNDER the escort of six men ostentatiously encumbered with rifles as well as revolvers, four cattlemen were thrust into the sweaty, crowded saloon.

The four were of a kind to command Kit's instant attention, contrasting with the sheepherders as white is to black. They were aristocrats as certainly as dukes and kings, possessing a pride of bearing and cleanness of feature bred by lifetimes in the saddle as lords of a vast domain. They were dressed in checkered shirts and flaring batwings and their spurs jingle-bobbed as they were marched forward. Their arms had been pinioned to their sides and their holsters were empty—facts which did not make them hide their contempt.

The entrance was met with catcalls, and an empty bottle swooshed out of the crowd to thump solidly into the side of the first in line. He was an older man, hair silvered by wind and scorching sun, and his years had taught him nothing if not forbearance. The blow must have been painful but he did not so much as glance at the hurler.

Plummer blocked their way before the bar, hooking his fingers into his cartridge belt and surveying them with an evil grin. "Well, Steele, still full of fight?"

The older man looked through Plummer.

Rainbow was angry. "How the hell did you do that?" he snapped at Plummer. "Damn it, I'm the only law officer in this county empowered to make arrests. I tell you that this is a court of justice!"

"Sure it is," replied Plummer easily. "And that's what we're goin' to have—justice! Line 'em up along here, boys. You, Whitey," he said, indicating the leader of the guard, "you're the first witness. Spill it to His Honor."

Whitey, an ugly, lumpy fellow, squared around with more than a hint of swagger. "I seen these four gents runnin' off sheep and shootin' 'em. And when I come up to stop 'em, they cut loose at me."

Carruthers tried to make a protest, but Plummer had released the wolves. "Next witness!"

A spindly, half-drunk fellow got up from the front row, holding on to his chair to keep from falling down. "I seen all four of these gents try to ambush two of us when we was carryin' supplies into our camp. We beat it and they ran off our flocks." He repressed a hiccup and sat down, looking all around him with a proud grin. Two or three slapped him on the back.

"Next!" thundered Plummer.

A big fellow with an expressionless face stood up. "There stands the four fellers that shot Dewey and Texas Dave. I seen it and I'd know 'em anywhere."

"Next!" shouted Plummer.

Carruthers twisted unhappily in his chair. "Really, Mr. Plummer, I can't accept any testimony unless the witnesses are sworn. I—"

"Next!" shouted Plummer, louder than before.

A nondescript hobo slunk forward and eyed the floor. "These gents busted up our bunch over by Rio Plata and shot . . ." He stopped, as uncertainly as a boy in a play who has forgotten his lines.

"Shot Greaser Charlie and Dog-Face Simpson," said Plummer.

"Yeah," said the hobo.

Through it all, the four cattlemen remained impassive. Steele's eyes were an electric and dangerous blue but he would not let out his wrath and so amuse this rabble. Kit knew he would go down without a murmur. A patch of dried blood on Steele's thigh showed that he had already done his best.

"Now all you gents," said Plummer, "ain't sworn to no testimony. Is everything you've told His Honor here the whole truth and nothin' but the truth so help you God?"

"Yeah," chorused the witnesses.

"There," said Plummer, turning to Carruthers. "You got the evidence against these four rannies. Steele and Martin and Thomas and Lancaster. We got witnesses and they've been proved guilty of murder. . . ."

"But," said Carruthers, "a jury trial—"

"We got a jury," said Plummer. "That second row is it and the gent on the end, Dawson, is the foreman. Now you satisfied, Judge?" The question was spaced with such a deadly meaning that Carruthers subsided helplessly, sinking deeper into his chair.

It was Rainbow who wanted a fight. "Plummer," he said, "you're too damned smart for your britches. This stuff won't stick for ten minutes and you know it. You got your pack of hound dogs bayin' to back you up and because you're faster'n most men on the draw, you're kingpin. You know doggone well that you found dough enough someplace to finance this here exodus into Yancy County. You got sheep and you got men. But that don't mean that you can pull off no reign of terror while I'm still swinging a gun. *Lex talionis—*"

"You got warrants," said Plummer, "for me and half a dozen of my boys. You ain't served 'em, Rainbow."

"I didn't serve them because you killed my deputy and then turned your mongrels loose on me. But if you're asking for it, Kettle-Belly Plummer, you're goin' to get it!" He yanked the sheaf of warrants from his pocket and slapped them down on the bar. In his right hand he held his Colt. "They're served and they include charges of everything from murder to arson."

"Rainbow," said Plummer with an unconcerned smile, "you got these out because you was elected to office by the cattle interests. There's your cattle interests," he laughed, jerking a scornful thumb at the four. "And I think, Rainbow, that I ought to indict a charge of false arrest right here and now. Early in the scrap you shot it out with a couple of my boys."

"What of it?" said Jackson.

"Witness!" shouted Plummer.

The hobo shoved himself to his feet again. His stage fright was over now and he grinned, delighted at the picture he thought he made, sorry scarecrow that he was. "I seen that. Lafferty and Sweeney was goin' along, mindin' their own business, and this here Jackson up and shot both of them from behind because they was sheepherders."

He sat down amid cheers.

Rainbow Jackson was struck dumb with rage and incredulity. The instant of inaction was enough. From behind him two men, who had crawled unseen around the ends of the bar, grabbed him and sent his Colt flying.

With a surge of strength, Jackson hurled them both back, shattering the mirror. He leaped through the haze of raining glass and over the bar, but his flight was short.

Plummer brought down the butt of a six-gun on Jackson's head and the big man dropped with a thud which made the building shudder.

Plummer reversed his gun with a careless flip and slid it into his holster. The two original attackers were picking themselves up, gashed and bleeding from amid a sea of spilled whiskey. They gladly obeyed Plummer's commanding gesture to drag Jackson aside.

Kit had been on the verge of acting but his hands had stopped halfway to his Colts. Here in these confines he courted suicide and he did not fancy dying in tatters. He knew what would happen now and into his mind sprang a plan which had only one chance in a thousand of succeeding. He looked at the four cattlemen and the inert Jackson and prayed for luck as he had never prayed before.

Plummer's stage was set. He faced Carruthers. "Okay, Your Honor. You want a verdict from the jury?"

Carruthers quailed. "No . . . wait. I . . ."

"You heard me," said Plummer.

Carruthers was completely wilted. "Yes."

"Dawson," said Plummer, "as foreman of the jury, what's the verdict?"

Dawson stood up. "The jury finds these four rannies guilty of murder and also the sheriff and recommends hangin' in the first degree."

"Okay," said Plummer. "And now, Judge, you got to agree with that sentence."

"No!" wailed Carruthers.

Plummer almost crushed the small man's shoulder with his grip and Carruthers knew that death was near. For a moment he tried to fight and then, finally, he broke.

"Yes," he whimpered.

As he turned, Plummer's white-fanged grin and murderous black eyes infected the mob and upon each face in the room, according to its capability for viciousness, something of that expression was stamped.

The four cattlemen exchanged a brief glance among themselves and again faced the crowd. Unflinching, hard of jaw, they prepared to meet death.

"Okay, boys," said Plummer.

The throng surged toward the bar, eagerly snatching at the cattlemen to thrust them from hand to rougher hand toward the front of the saloon. Rainbow Jackson, reviving, was kicked into motion and thrown back and forth through the mob like a huge polo ball.

Carruthers sat slumped in his seat, unmoving and unseeing, head fallen forward on his chest. Plummer gave him one last contemptuous glance and then strode forward with his jackals.

It was time for Kit to be going, but a crowd had collected outside and his going was impeded. Before he realized it, Plummer was behind him, shoving him harshly to one side.

Kit stared straight at the gunman, tensed for action, but Plummer did not penetrate the disguise and strode out into the blinding sunlight.

Holding his own against the wall, Kit let the crowd jostle into the street. Their voices dinned savagely through Gunsmoke. They were in high spirits and their laughter was a steady roar as they booted their luckless captives along.

Among the last to leave were Rainbow and his tormentors. The guards were having trouble in removing him as Rainbow was fighting all the way, laying big hands on everything he could reach.

The sheepherders got him to the door but he grabbed the casement and resisted with all his strength, bellowing like a wounded grizzly. Suddenly he caught sight of Kit against the wall.

"Mason!" gasped Jackson. "Get out before they kill you too!"

The guards won out and Jackson was hurled, still fighting, into the street to be instantly buried under a gleeful pile of greasy shirts and hard muscles.

Kit watched with compressed lips and then, turning, strode across the wrecked saloon, slid out through the window and to the ground. Carefully he scanned his way and then made a rush for the rickety building which bore the sign, "Longhorn Hotel."

Chapter Six

THE lobby was apparently deserted when Kit Gordon cat-footed watchfully across it. Here the din was muffled but sounding more deadly for that.

As Kit breasted the counter a clerk timidly exposed one eye around the end of the safe and, seeing only one man, presented the other and then his bald head complete.

"Come out of there!" said Kit. "Where is Plummer's room?"

"I . . . ah . . ." The clerk cast a frightened glance toward the street. Through the fly-smudged windows he could see the crowd uproariously marching their victims toward a lone oak which stood, bare and scorched, upon the edge of Gunsmoke. Ropes were prominently displayed and the bared heads of the captives were all that could be seen over the mob.

"Plummer's room!" said Kit impatiently.

The clerk was hesitant. He had lived a life of terror for three weeks, since the day Plummer had arrived and taken his residence there. Fear of consequences made him tremble.

Kit solved the difficulty by whipping the ink-spattered register around and turning back a page so swiftly that he tore it. There it was: Plummer, Number Ten.

Kit shoved the register back at the clerk, catching the fellow in the stomach and slamming him down on the floor.

"Stay where you are," said Kit Gordon, "and speak to nobody."

Running, he mounted the stairs, pausing at the top only long enough to spot "Number Ten" in the dim hall.

He cared little whether or not the door was locked. He raised his foot and slammed his heel against the keyhole, shattering the lock and wrenching the door half from its hinges.

The interior was cluttered with clothing and gear and Kit took a swift survey of Plummer's stacked baggage before he ripped into it.

At the bottom of the pile he found a saddlebag which was too heavy. He slapped up the straps and looked within. Both sides were filled with gold coins still in their paper rolls. Another bag was crammed with securities on a San Francisco bank. Under this, wrapped in a blanket, was a sack of registered mail, still unopened.

Kit stood up, throwing the articles back with an angry toss. He yanked a suitcase from under the bed and pried it open. The first article which he welcomed was his own white Stetson, the spare which Plummer had stolen from the hotel in the north.

Under the hat lay Kit's clothing, folded carefully for future reference, even including a pair of Gordon's boots.

The shouting had grown less distinct and a glance down at the street showed Kit that the mob had arrived at the oak and were very busy with the preliminaries.

Knowing how small was his margin of time, Kit tore the rags from him and cast swiftly about for Plummer's shaving gear. He sloshed water into the big china bowl and hastily scrubbed lather into the tangled hair on his face. Without any regard for the tenderness of his skin, he whipped off the whiskers with an open-edged razor.

As he dressed he watched the progress of the multiple hanging. The crowd was falling over itself, making a Roman holiday with mirth and horseplay. They had Rainbow up on a mustang and the sheriff was battling back all he could despite his lashed arms. Above the tumult, Jackson's thundering voice strove to condemn them all to eternal fire. The mob was jostling him and pelting him and replying with wit low enough to find ready acceptance with the throng.

Another group had Steele on a horse. Impassively, he watched them placing a hangman's noose about his throat while two men tried to throw the other end over a gallows bough.

Kit buttoned his beautifully tailored coat and then buckled his gunbelts around it on the outside. He lashed down his holsters and loosened his Colts.

Pulling his white Stetson aslant over his lean face, he glanced in the cracked mirror as if to make certain that he looked like himself again.

At the edge of town, the crowd had succeeded in placing Steele's rope and were now goading Steele's horse up under the bough. They had put the noose around Jackson's neck and were making ready to get him into position.

Kit sped from the room and clattered down the steps. As he passed the desk the clerk looked blankly at him, wondering if he could be the same fellow who had gone up. And then something clicked in the clerk's mind. The white Stetson, the black frock coat, the flowing tie and linen shirt, the lustrous boots and tied-down guns . . .

Paralyzed in earnest this time, the clerk watched Kit Gordon stride into the sunbaked street.

Kit paused for an instant on the high boardwalk before he stepped down. He knew that one man could do very little against that crowd, reputation or no. But he had to go, had to try. . . .

"Jesus!" said somebody in a window at his back. "It's . . . it's Suicide Gordon!"

Kit whirled. An old man, bearing the unmistakable and clean stamp of the puncher, was standing inside one of the hotel rooms on the bottom floor. The man had a drooping white mustache and wore a Stetson with flaring brim.

"Mr. Gordon, I . . . Look, what are you going to do?" He blinked at Kit on the sidewalk. "Look, I'm Cass Shannon of the Triangle Bar. I seen you in Dodge when you and Plummer swapped lead. . . ."

Kit nodded, his mind on the crowd and the hanging which was about to proceed.

"Look," said Shannon, "you'd commit suicide if you walked into that gang. Me'n about twenty of the boys come simmering in here, but we can't do nothing to save Steele and Jackson an' . . . It's suicide!"

Kit began to smile with cold calculation. "You want to do something?" He looked up the street and saw that a water trough was in the middle of the road, some hundred feet this side of the oak.

"Y'mean there is something us boys can do?"

"Yes," said Kit. "I'm going to walk up there and if they don't get me first, you men scatter through these buildings and stand ready to help."

"You bet," said Shannon. "All we needed was somebody to kind of head us right!"

Kit stepped down off the high boardwalk and into the center of the road. He slowed down as he began his march toward the oak tree.

A crew had laid hold of the ropes. Two men prepared to slap the mounts of Jackson and Steele with quirts.

Kit strode slowly, his hands swinging free, his eyes as gray and clear as a wolf's. He was all alone in the center of that deserted street, a single dapper figure, marching with a stride which clearly indicated that only death itself could stop him.

The babble of the mob grew louder until it was like a steady physical impact. Coarse voices were bellowing to Jackson and Steele, telling them blasphemous messages to give to the Devil.

They had not seen Kit Gordon. Not yet.

Plummer was standing on a box, directing the proceedings, shouting, "When I say three, give them hosses hell! One . . ." He was looking up at Jackson and for once the sheriff was silent, his beard parted in a snarl of contempt. Plummer was enjoying the sport.

Kit kept walking. The outskirts of the rabble was thirty, twenty-nine, twenty-eight paces. Twenty-seven, twenty-six . . .

A man on the edge to Kit's right saw him coming and stopped moving to stare. The tallest of the rope crew broke off in the middle of a raucous laugh.

"Two," shouted Plummer.

A mounted man, the hobo, caught sight of the gaping crewman and turned to freeze at the sight of Kit.

Twenty paces away from the edge, all alone in the heat waves which beat upward from the hot sand, Kit stopped.

The roar was undiminished at first, but then man after man noticed the stilled postures of the rope man, the mounted hobo and the fellow on the edge. One by one, as a snuffer caps out candles, voices broke off. Gradually at first, then faster, the din lessened.

A mass of snaggletoothed mouths and tangled hair and misshapen faces were whipping around toward Kit.

And then a voice, hushed with awe, whispered, "Suicide Gordon!"

Kit made no move. Tall and alone, he watched them spinning about to face him, watched the sun glittering on gun barrels held in momentarily motionless hands.

And then the name echoed like a shudder through the rabble. For seconds not even a dust mote moved in the hot afternoon.

Plummer, staring over the heads of his men, the "three" unuttered upon his lips, went suddenly stiff and his black eyes grew as metallic as iron.

Kit had made no move toward his guns. He left it to Plummer to do that.

Plummer's tongue flicked out to moisten his lips. In that instant he could not call out to his men and so lose his prestige. And, again, this man was meat for his own guns.

Plummer's voice crackled through the electric silence. "Well?"

"Draw," said Kit Gordon, hard and slow.

Plummer's hand blurred and three shattering reports blasted almost together. White smoke swirled in a billowing cloud before Plummer.

No man had seen Gordon's hands move. But the guns were there, smoke drooling from their muzzles.

The hardness faded from Plummer's eyes to be replaced by a look of growing surprise. The Colt in his stiff right hand turned around on its trigger guard and fell off his finger. He clutched in abrupt agony at his stomach and collapsed from view.

Not until that instant did the crowd realize its own strength, realize that one man stood here before them by the water trough, a clear target for any gun.

And guns flashed into the sunlight. . . .

But Kit Gordon vanished.

He dropped into the dust behind the trough's cover and half a hundred bullets fanned the air where he had been. The water in the trough began to geyser and suddenly the wood was like a sieve under the hammering fusillade.

Kit did not show himself. The crowd, grown bold through noise, began to yell and surge ahead to flank the trough and crack down for the kill.

And Kit heard them come above the snap and whine of lead over him.

But another sound joined the melee.

Twenty rifles began to roar as fast as men could lever cartridges into smoking chambers, sight and pull lead.

The mob had been too intent upon Gordon. From nowhere,

or so it seemed to them, a volley was hacking them down like tenpins.

In a space of thirty seconds the entire front of the rabble was down in the street. In sudden panic, staring wide-eyed into the town and seeing white smoke leaping from the windows along the street, every man in the crowd thought of nothing but his own safety.

They whirled, Gordon forgotten, racing anywhere as long as they could get out of range.

The barrage was going over Gordon's head, but he raised himself up and, with nice precision, took the perjurers down as they sprinted, turned, fired and fell prone in the dirt.

The shattering volleys continued from the street. There was no safety in town. There was no leader now in the crowd.

They were running like the sheep they herded and, at last, did not even stop to return the fire.

And then they were gone into the gullies of the plain, and behind them the sod was strewn with their members and weapons dropped to make the running better.

And out of the hotels and saloons dashed the twenty punchers to help cut the bonds of Jackson and the other four.

The cowmen, yelling and exultant, clustered about the quintet who had become so nearly corpses.

"That's takin' 'em!" yelled Shannon. "I never seen such nerve!"

And another cowman crowed, "We've licked sheep forever in Yancy County. They won't never come back now that Plummer's dead!"

Kit flipped his guns into the air and caught them in his

palms to slide them into his holsters. Quietly he walked up to Jackson and unclasped a knife to swiftly slice away his bonds.

Nobody had anything to say, too full were they of relief. Kit released all five before anyone spoke. And then it was Steele.

"There comes that goddamned judge."

Rainbow Jackson scratched his bushy black beard and took his eyes from the approaching figure.

"You're Suicide Gordon," said the sheriff. "Wanted for train robbery and murder." His voice made it into an amazed question.

Kit stirred the lump at his feet which was—or had been—Kettle-Belly Plummer. "You'll find the evidence about that in this gent's hotel room. He wanted to invest his money in sheep and by spotting me, he put himself in the clear."

Rather awed, Rainbow nodded, seeing light. He cleared his throat uneasily. "No wonder you was so good with that left-hand gun," he said irrelevantly.

Steele had been pulling himself together. "Mr. Gordon, I reckon it sounds kind of silly to tell you thanks. I was wondering if you could stick around as a sort of special officer. I . . ."

Kit gave Jackson a wicked grin and jerked his thumb at the plodding Carruthers. "I believe, Steele, that your sheriff here would rather depend upon what he calls *lex scripta,* law by the statute."

"Aw, hell," writhed Jackson, "that just went for most ornery lawmen like me. I take it back. *Lex talionis* is the medicine this country needs. How the hell was I to know it was goin' to be applied by the greatest gunman of 'em all, huh?"

Carruthers arrived, panting with congratulations, and the four cattlemen chimed in, pressing their offer.

But Kit was not listening. From Plummer's pocket he took his repeater watch, gazing at it fondly. He pressed the small button on the side and notes like crystal bells floated in the air: *bing, bing-bing, ting.*

The No-Gun Gunhawk

Chapter One

H E did not know, when he rode out to the edge of the plain, that he was looking down the abyss of trouble, and that he was about to take the long dive himself. In fact, nothing was further from Pete McClean's mind at the moment, and to testify that he was a peaceable man, he did not wear a gun.

It looked up to that point that his dad had been right and that he had been right. The best way to keep out of war was to keep away from guns, and that theory, considering the times, was at least novel.

But the thing he saw out there in the bright Montana sunshine was puzzling. A man who glittered like a Christmas tree and who carried his left arm in a sling was sitting on a black horse and talking to a girl. Pete McClean knew better than to intrude and he was not close enough to hear. He remained masked by the coulee. He hadn't come all the way from the Panhandle to Roundup to run into a war.

Less than a hundred yards from them, Pete could see that the girl was strikingly different from any other girl he had ever seen. She was dressed in a split riding skirt and a white silk shirt. She wore small spurred boots of beautifully tooled leather, and gauntlets which were fringed and beaded Indian style. Her flat-topped, straight-brimmed Stetson sat at a cocky angle upon her tawny hair.

And even at that short distance, McClean could see that she was very angry.

The man she faced had his back to Pete. And then, when the man turned to point south, Pete saw that he was masked.

The fact was startling. The girl looked lovely and innocent and she was talking to a masked rider with the attitude an employer takes toward his employed.

"Better keep out of this," muttered Pete to himself.

Pete neck-reined back into the coulee and started north again, riding slowly and silently without raising any dust. It was no business of his and in these times a man did well to keep away from such things. Pete was peaceable.

He thought about it in the next hour, rather saddened by the sight. Something was afoot. Perhaps he had better pass up Roundup and go further north into the Milk River country. He had a definite premonition that the thing he had witnessed would somehow concern him.

His buckskin scented water with a toss of his head and presently they came across a small creek bordered with willows. The buckskin began to drink noisily and Pete threw himself down on the gravel to follow that excellent example.

An ice-cold voice sounded on the other side of the stream.

"Howdy, stranger. Don't bother movin' none."

Pete raised himself to his hands and knees. About ten feet away a very flashy gentleman was standing behind long-snouted Colts, which he balanced easily. A red bandana with two eye slits obscured the fellow's face. It was the same man who had been talking to the girl.

"What's the matter?" said Pete, aggrieved. "Am I poaching on this private crick of yours?"

The gentleman's eyes glared. "Stand up and shed your irons and no tricks."

Pete stood up and, with a start, the gentleman saw that the young puncher was not armed.

"What the hell? You ain't packin' a hawg laig?"

"It's a good way to keep out of trouble," said Pete.

"Huh, that's what you think. What's your name?"

"McClean."

"McClean? Don't give me that. You're too young to be Tad McClean and he never went without a gun nowheres. Go on, put up your paws and don't be so damned fidgety."

"Tad McClean was my father."

"I doubt it. No fighter like Tad McClean ever had a son that wouldn't fight."

"He made me . . . I came west to find him and finally located him in Texas. He's still there."

"The hell you preach. Come on, keep up your hands. Do you think I'm doin' this for amusement? How's that?"

"I buried him," said Pete, "after his last gunfight."

"Couldn't have been an even break," said the gentleman. "Nobody ever beat Tad to the draw. *Nobody.*"

"No? That's what he thought. But they did and it was all fair. I saw it."

"And lit out?"

"Not exactly," said Pete. "I drilled the man that did it."

"And his friends . . . ?"

"No," said Pete. "The man didn't have no friends, but Texas didn't look so good."

"Then if you killed the man that beat Tad McClean to an even break—huh, I can't understand it. And not packin' a gun. I can't understand it at all. What's the matter?"

"Gunslingers die hard," said Pete. "There's no use of it. Gunslingers will never build up the West, they'll tear it down. My dad was a fast one, the best of the lot, and where did it get him? He's in Boot Hill."

"I get it. Yellow."

Pete flared, "No, I'm not yellow, but I'm not a gunfighter and I'll never be one, and the safest way to keep out of trouble is leave your gun in your war sack and mind your own business."

"Is that so?" said the gentleman. "I don't know how you figure that out. Judge Colt is ruling everything west of the Mississippi and so many men can't be wrong. I'll give you some advice, son. Buckle on your iron after I leave you. This country ain't healthy for men that don't shoot first and talk afterwards. I get your point. Your dad got snuffed out and soured you on the trade. Huh, well, daylight's burning. Shuck your duds."

"My duds?" said Pete, failing to understand.

"Climb out of your clothes and fast. I haven't got all day."

"And if I don't?"

"Then I'll have to undress a corpse."

Pete looked into the unwavering muzzles and then into the cold eyes buried in the mask. He said something and didn't smile when he said it. He began to climb out of his clothes.

First he took off his boots, then his pants, then his shirt

and vest and finally his wide-brimmed, flat-topped Texas hat and laid it upon the pile.

The gentleman forded the creek on stones. "I'd be smarter if I killed you, McClean, but I've got a use for you. Here, you can put these on. I haven't any use for them. Won them in a stud game and thought they was pretty, but . . ."

He took off his stamped boots and his silver Spanish spurs and pegged them at Pete. Then he removed the "chinkies" which were tooled with color and bore several pounds of Spanish conchas about their belt and down their flaring legs. He shed his holsters which sparkled in the warm Montana sun and tossed them to Pete. Finally he slipped out of his silver-braided vest and passed that over. As an afterthought, he removed his hat with its beaded and sparkling chin thong and passed that over.

This was all a riddle to Pete, why any man should want to part with such foofaraw was quite beyond him. He was amazed when the gentleman began sliding into Pete's worn batwings and ragged checkered shirt and threadbare vest. He realized then that they were of a similar size, both being lanky.

Except for the red bandana, there stood Pete McClean. "Now dress," said the gentleman.

Pete dressed, handling the shiny rig as though it would bite him. When he had finished he stepped over and looked at himself in a quiet backwater of the creek and was quite shocked at his flashy appearance. In fact, he took a little pride in all these silver trappings, and in those flappy, colored "chinkies."

He looked at the gentleman. "You mean I can keep these?"

"Sure, kid. Keep them and welcome. You look right nice in them. You ain't a bad-lookin' kid and it's too bad you don't like guns. Your arms is all loose-like and might be pretty fast and while you ain't exactly got a poker face, bein' so young, that ain't sayin' you couldn't develop it in time. Well, I might have looked like that once."

The gentleman, still holding a Colt on Pete, backed across the stream and led a jaded horse out of the brush. Lather had dried white on the silky coat and the horse stumbled as it was led. But what Pete saw was the saddle. His own was a plain macheer, the utmost in utility and the minimum in design. This saddle was Mexican, all glittering with great round silver conchas which outlined the cantle and skirts. The horn was also silver.

"This is Ginger," said the gentleman. "And now, young fellow, don't say I didn't give you an even swap."

He took Pete's comparatively fresh horse and mounted up, wincing when he twisted his bandaged shoulder.

"My advice, youngster, is that you get the hell out of here and go north. Keep away from the gullies, and keep away from Roundup. Adios."

The gentleman splashed across the stream and disappeared up a coulee, leaving Pete quite dazed behind him.

"I'll be a son of a gun," said Pete. "I can't make nothin' out of it at all."

He mounted the black Ginger and neck-reined him down the ravine. Time and again he looked at his shadow and the way the conchas battered the sunlight up against the gray rocks. He was somewhat pleased with his rig because his own clothes had almost been worn out.

The holsters were empty, of course, but they made a show just the same. Tad McClean, down in Boot Hill, would never have approved of that, but his son was quite content, true to his vow that he would never be classed as a gunslinger and would never pack a gun.

And then the little devils of the air that prey on men's destinies began to get to work. When Pete emerged into a long stretch he heard:

Ka-pow! Ka-pow!

A bullet clipped off a stone and shrilled viciously up into the blue.

Somewhere in the hills to his left the rifle sounded again: *Ka-pow!* Hollow and faint with distance.

Pete dug in the silver spurs and began to ride.

Chapter Two

AS Pete rolled the plain back under the faltering hoofs of Ginger, he stabbed a glance over his shoulder toward the canyons which yawned like gunsights along the hills behind him.

It began to rain horsemen. They came headlong out of the draws, low over their horns, quirts crackling to the rushing undertone of rolling hoofs. It seemed to Pete that a whole regiment of cavalry was upon him.

Dust rolled up in a great yellow fog toward the blue. The sun struck on gun barrels. Men's voices brayed like trumpets for Pete to stop.

Pete thought that he had better keep going. He laid on with his quirt and jabbed home his spurs and prayed that his weary horse could keep up the pace.

With a feeling of terror he realized that it was a long way across the flat and that he was mounted on a horse which had already come far that day.

But Ginger tried, thrusting out his sleek neck and flaring his nostrils until the wind whistled past them.

Odd dust geysers began to spout on Pete's course, to the right and left. He was under heavy fire which, though not accurate, was annoying.

For a rage-filled instant he wished that he had a rifle. He'd clear a few of those saddles before they cleared his. And then he remembered that guns were the root of all evil and felt ashamed of himself.

If Ginger could make the far range of hills he might be able to thoroughly lose himself. There was a chance that he could get across before a bullet plucked him out of leather.

What the hell did all those gents want, anyway?

Then he knew that it was his clothes. He had fallen for an old gag like that. He was a sucker. It did not enter his head that he had been far from choosing in the matter. His clothes were the target, not Pete. No wonder that gentleman had seen fit to swap this expensive rig for a plain one. That gentleman had been very, very wise.

Oh, well, when they caught up to him they'd see right away that he was the wrong man.

He started to slacken his pace and then knew that they might nail him without an argument. Again he applied his quirt and the fan of horseflesh and powder flame behind him came closer.

Less than a mile away Pete could see another coulee. He would get into that and all would be well. Ginger was getting his second wind.

Pete began to put a wider margin between himself and his pursuers. It looked as though he could make it and get away and then, the wind devils, hearing his plea, put their thumbs down.

Ginger's forefoot went into a gopher hole.

The whole world did a back flip. Lying upon the downy cushion of air, Pete noticed with a shock that all the mountains were upside down and that he appeared to be falling into the sky. Then the mountains flipped again and Pete looked a prickly pear in the spiny eye and the lights flared and went out.

Drag him to his feet, damn it. He ain't dead, God help him."

Pete stared up at a black hat which perched over a frowning, thick face. Two close-set black eyes were boring into him and a gun muzzle indicated his middle.

Two men were dismounted and the rest had drawn into a tight, gun-studded ring about Pete. Ginger was cropping at bunch grass and limping a little, outside the circle.

A bowlegged, sour-faced matchstick was holding Pete up with the help of another who was six feet tall and almost as thick. These two shook Pete a little just to show him that they could.

"String him up, Teed," cried somebody in the crowd.

"Hell," said Teed, "what would Roundup say if we didn't let them in on the fun? We're vigilantes, and as such if we don't obey the law and string him to that big cottonwood for everybody to see, then who the hell will obey us, huh?"

The bowlegged one glanced across Pete at his mate. "He don't look so tough, Rainy. I thought he was supposed to look hard."

Rainy shook his head wisely. "You never can tell about these gents. He looks like a babe but that don't say he ain't killed goin' on fifteen men."

"He won't kill anymore," said Teed, glaring hard at Pete. "Load him up, boys, and we'll take him back to Roundup."

"Wait a minute," said Pete. "You gents are dead wrong.

69

I'm not the guy you want. The man you want made me take these clothes and—"

A roar of laughter lapped up and silenced his words.

"Don't tell me," said Teed. "You've throwed lead just once too often. If you had a kind heart you wouldn't begrudge us the pleasure of hangin' you, Tornado."

"I'm not any tornado," cried Pete, whipping his blood-matted blond hair out of his gray eyes. "I'm a peaceable gent and my name's McClean."

"His name's McClean and he's a peaceable gent," said Rainy, shaking his small head sorrowfully. "Hell's afire, cowboy, didn't nobody ever teach you how to lie? Mungo here could do better than that, dumb as he is."

"But look at my face," cried Pete. "I'm not the man you want."

"That's what we're doing," said Teed. "Lookin' at your face. And I'm guessin' that we're the first men to see the Tornado unmasked. Them clothes stamp you, Tornado McClean."

"No," yelled Pete. "My name's Pete McClean."

"Or maybe," added the thin scarecrow called Mungo, "or maybe it's Tad McClean we've heard so much about."

"Come on," said an impatient rider, "cut out the palaver. It's time enough for a powwow when we get to Roundup."

"Listen," began Pete. "I just drifted up from Texas and down the line a ways a gent stuck—"

"Tie him to his saddle," ordered Teed.

They boosted the protesting Pete up to his saddle and lashed his hands to the horn and then, leading his horse, they started south toward Roundup.

"You might at least tell me," said Pete, "what you think I did."

Teed, riding on his right, snorted loudly. "I suppose you got amnesia or something of the sort. I suppose you didn't remember walkin' out into the street and shootin' down Hastings, my cashier, from behind."

"Listen," pleaded Pete. "I'm plumb peaceable. I just drifted up from Texas and I'll admit that I'm Tad McClean's son. But I don't even pack a gun, see?"

"Throwed 'em away," volunteered Rainy, with an ugly scowl.

"They sure was beauties," added Mungo. "I seen you when you downed Hastings and—"

Teed was interested in other things. He said, "How much was old Donnelly payin' you, McClean?"

"Donnelly?" said Pete. "Who's he?"

"You mean," said Rainy, patiently, "that you didn't know who hired you? You didn't know Donnelly owns the biggest spread up here?"

"He's fakin'," said Mungo sourly.

"I might ask," said Pete, "how come you gents are so suddenly spurred on by justice?"

Rainy, in a painfully patient voice, said, "We're vigilantes, young feller. We're bringin' law and order to these parts. Roundup ain't goin' to suffer no more from you evildoers. This is all legal-like and perfectly proper and the gent that says it ain't is goin' to get plugged plenty."

After that, aside from scowls in his direction, they left him alone, and late in the afternoon they rode into Roundup.

People streamed out of stores and stood on the boardwalks and pointed. An old man in a red shirt who used a Sharps for a crutch cried, "Hurray for the vigilantes!"

71

The group stopped in front of the California Saloon—which was directly across the street from the New York Store—and began to dismount, holding Pete with the muzzles of many threatening six-guns.

"Come on, you rannies," cried Teed. "Anybody that wants to see a first-class hangin' step right this way."

The crowd in the street consisted of punchers and miners and gamblers and dance-hall girls and barkeeps and several men whose flowered vests, nugget watch chains, black frock coats and small hats stamped them as the leading citizens. One and all, they regarded Pete with lustful eyes.

"Hurray for the vigilantes!" cried the old man in the red shirt, waving his Sharps.

The crowd bawled it over and over, and then, flanking Pete's horse, began to push and drag the animal down toward a big cottonwood which stood on the edge of the rickety town. A dozen punchers were fighting to offer their ropes and then one of them settled it by dropping a neat loop over Pete's neck.

"Hurray for law and order!" roared a miner.

Teed sat back in his saddle and grinned evilly. Mungo and Rainy exchanged sly glances and the rest of the posse rode sourly like men with a purpose.

They came out of the waning sunlight and into the shadow of the broad limbs and the puncher whose rope graced Pete's neck made another expert toss over the limb.

"Untie his hands, the murderer," yelled the puncher.

Teed wanted to do that himself and he had almost reached Pete when an angry voice cut through the roar of the throng.

Pete glanced over his shoulder and was startled to behold the girl he had seen talking to the Tornado. She was spurring forward through the press, pushing men to either side.

Teed saw her coming and tightened his thin mouth into a grimace.

"Look here, Miss Sally," said Teed. "Get out and let men do their duty. This is no business of yours."

"It's the business of the citizens," said Sally Donnelly, thrusting Teed's hand off her rein. "Men! Do you call this justice? Are you going to blacken the name of Roundup by a lynching just as soon as you have elected these vigilantes?"

The miners and punchers and townspeople looked up at her through the hot dust and stared. She was white with rage and her eyes flamed at them. Another hand tried to take her rein and she struck at the blurred face with her quirt.

"What about the trial?" demanded Sally Donnelly.

The miners and the punchers took it up. The old man in the red shirt waved his Sharps and yelled, "Hell, we forgot the trial. We got to have this regular. Where's Judge Larsen?"

Teed made his braying voice heard above them. "There isn't any use tryin' the murderer. We all know he did it. We all saw him shoot down Hastings in cold blood. Stretch that rope, cowboy!"

"No!" yelled the crowd, suddenly placing themselves with a girl whose beauty was a strange thing to find in such a wild country. "Where's Judge Larsen?"

"He won't be back until morning!" cried Teed. "We ain't got anyplace to keep a prisoner. String him up."

"Men! Do you call this justice?
Are you going to blacken the name of Roundup by a lynching
just as soon as you have elected these vigilantes?"

The old man in the red shirt yelled, "What's the matter with your vault? That's the place! We got to have a trial!"

Teed tried again to make himself heard, but Miss Sally Donnelly had turned the trick against him. He glared at her like a rattler about to strike and even rested his hand upon the butt of his shoulder gun which, though he certainly did not intend to use it on her, indicated his feelings.

After several minutes of argument, Rainy and Mungo, seeing that their boss was talked down, led Pete away toward the granite-walled bank.

Pete, dazed by all this, and more dazed because of the girl's sudden appearance than because he had escaped being hanged, looked back at Sally Donnelly. He expected her to smile at him, but in that he was wrong.

She was eyeing him with a glare of which a cougar might have been proud. Sheer hate was in her eyes. Pete gulped and faced the bank again.

If she had rescued him, then why did she hate him? And if . . . So that was it. She was in cahoots with a murderer and she was somehow in the Tornado's power. But why, if that were the case, had she bothered about it at all?

It was a sorry puzzle and Pete was too engrossed in it to notice that they had thrust him into the vault and had closed the brass grate upon him.

"Sit still and silent," said Mungo, his narrow face set and menacing. "If you try anything at all, I'll let air and sunlight into you."

Pete seated himself on a Wells Fargo box and somberly began to figure things out.

Chapter Three

MIDNIGHT and Rainy came and Mungo went away. Rainy peered through the brass grate at Pete.

"You better be contemplatin' your sins," said Rainy, filling up the whole opening with his broad, tall bulk. "Judge Larsen is gettin' all set for the trial and he says you ought to hang proper-like. But Holy Joe refused to come over and console you, him bein' too busy playin' stud at the Palace Saloon."

"Look here," said Pete, "can't I get a lawyer?"

"Lawyer? Lemme see. Lawyer. Oh, I remember now. We had a lawyer here but he wrote up a contract for Two-Finger Blane and Two-Finger lost out. The lawyer wa'nt good enough with a gun, I reckon, and we had to bury him. No, you can't have no lawyer, because there ain't none."

A window rattled, which was odd because there was no wind. Rainy turned around and picked up the lamp, going to the window. "Hey, who's that?"

Pete held his breath. But he had no great hopes. He had no friends here in Roundup and any claim he might have on men was through Tad McClean. And his dad's reputation had already carried its curse through the second generation.

Rainy came back to the vault. His thick, muscular face

was stamped with a frown. "I don't think anybody in their right senses would try nothin' while I was on the job," he decided.

The words were hardly out of his mouth when the bank resounded with a hollow crack. The frown smoothed itself on Rainy's face and was slowly replaced by a look of wonder. Rainy's mighty hulk began to melt down. With a clatter, he fell to the floor.

Astounded, Pete saw the old man in the red shirt standing in the yellow lamplight, still holding his Sharps by its muzzle.

"I guess that settles him," said the old one, dropping his Sharps into its more common office as a crutch. "You still in there? Wall, I'm Buzz Whitlaw, and Miss Sally is waitin' for ye."

Keys rattled and Pete stepped out of his cell. Buzz Whitlaw stumped to the window and poked out his head. "All right, Miss Sally."

Pete could see Ginger's silky coat in the starlight. The silver conchas were white blurs. Beyond Ginger, Pete could see the vague outline of the girl.

Pete scrambled over the sill, thrust his foot into a stirrup and swung aboard. Buzz Whitlaw dropped down with startling agility for one who only had one leg and gave Ginger a slap on the rump.

"Get out of town," said Buzz.

"But they'll think," began the girl, "they'll think you did it and—"

"Pshaw. Never mind me. I ain't forgot about Sam Donnelly's

boost last winter. You never mind about that. I'll be leading the vigilantes next time you see me."

The girl started off without a word to Pete. Ginger followed, hoofbeats muffled by the dust. They were going west from the sleeping cow town.

When he was sure that they were not being pursued, Pete ventured to speak to the girl.

"Thanks," said Pete. "I'd just about given up hope when—"

"What's that?"

"I said thanks for—"

"No, I mean your voice. It's different somehow. . . . But then, of course, you aren't wearing that mask you're so proud of. No need to talk, mister. Just ride. The less you say, the better I'll like it."

"Wait a minute," said Pete. "You've got me all wrong. I'm not the man you think I am. I'm not this gent they call the Tornado. I'm Pete McClean from down in the Panhandle."

The girl drew up and stared closely at him. Then she turned and went forward again. "I don't know what your point is, but you're certainly the man I think you are."

"But my voice," pleaded Pete. "Can't you tell by my voice?"

"Save it," said the girl. "Any man can shift his voice and I've only talked to you once before. Keep quiet and follow me."

"Look here," said Pete in desperation, "I'm Pete McClean and my dad was Tad McClean."

"I always wondered what your real name was."

"But listen," begged Pete, about to launch forth on an explanation of his peaceable intentions.

"It's no use. I know who you are and I fought Dad from the first when he insisted upon hiring you. Golden Valley won't be held by gunmen."

"Please," said Pete. "Tell me what this is all about."

"I suppose," replied Sally, sarcastically, "that you have no memory at all. I suppose Dad didn't hire you to fight Teed. I suppose you'll try to tell me again that you had nothing to do with killing Hastings but just went into the town to look over the ground."

"But I'm not this gent you think I am," cried Pete forlornly. "I'm just a puncher lookin' for peace and a job, that's all, and whatever the trouble is here, I have nothing at all to do with it. And if you—well, why did you save me from that lynch mob if you think me so terrible?"

"They arrested you because you were following Dad's orders. I can't let one of my father's men, no matter how low and ornery, be lynched because he carried out Dad's command. I don't know what this is all about, but I do know that I had to get you away from them for fear you'd tell them about Dad's plans. Now keep quiet or I'll take a shot at you myself."

Pete rode silently after that. From the nearby buttes he could hear the coyotes howling and moaning and yapping in dismal chorus. The black night was a velvet cloak about their shoulders and the stars sparkled overhead and, in other circumstances, Pete would have enjoyed this ride.

He had never seen a girl like this one and something kept telling him over and over that if he didn't straighten this out he would be sorry about it the rest of his life.

They were crossing a low range of hills, ragged black cardboard against the night. Ahead lay the lights in the ranch houses of Golden Valley.

Chapter Four

SAM DONNELLY'S first words of greeting were eager. "Did you get Teed?"

Pete stood upon the creaking boards of the rough floor and stared at the small, ashen-faced man who lay in a mound of blankets.

"Listen," said Pete. "Both you and your daughter have got me all wrong. I'm nobody but Pete McClean, and if you've ever seen this gent that styles himself the Tornado, you'll know I'm not him."

The old man looked closely up at Pete's face. "Your voice— Damn it, don't come in here with some cock-and-bull story like that. Just because you didn't have nerve enough to go through with it, don't lie. Speak up like a man, you lobo, and don't beat around the bush about it."

"I don't know what you mean," said Pete. "If you sent the Tornado to kill Teed, he didn't do it. He shot a man named Hastings and then got a slug in his own arm and lit out. He met me up on a crick—"

"Take him out of here," moaned Sam Donnelly, his small eyes blazing but sunken with weariness. "Take him out of here, Sally. You were right. I never should have hired the coyote in the first place."

"Wait a minute," begged Pete. "Maybe if you tell me just what the trouble is—"

"Again?" yelled Donnelly, springing up into a sitting posture and grabbing at his holstered Colts which hung on the bedpost. Then he thought better of it and sank back. Wearily, he said, "All right, I'll give you another chance."

"Don't," said Sally. "He isn't worth another chance." She gave Pete a disgusted glance and added, "When I met him he said he was wounded in the arm and couldn't fight that way and now he's forgotten all about it. I've got my opinion of men who look for alibis."

It so happened that Pete had just thought of that as a perfect explanation of his identity, but the girl had beaten him to it.

"Listen," said Sam Donnelly. "You can't fail me this time. I'm paying you good money to do this because the buzzards winged me twice and I can't do it, and they've scared off all my men. Teed wants Golden Valley, the biggest spread in these parts. Bein' the banker, he's tried to loan me money and get it that way. He doesn't dare go as far as to rustle my stock, but he'll do anything else he can."

Sam had the air of one who explains a simple lesson to a child for the tenth time. "Teed wants this land. He wants Golden Valley, but just how he can take it and make it stick I don't know. There are still white men in this country who won't let him kill me and then steal the place.

"But Teed has something up his sleeve. Perhaps— Oh, I don't know. I'm half-crazy thinking about this. I've got money, but since my punchers drifted out of here, scared off,

I suppose, I can't do anything. And I'm not going to leave Sally to these buzzards.

"There's only one answer, gunslinger, and that's the killing of Teed. You came whining to me, masked and worn out, and begged me to help you. You said you'd take the job and now you have it. Teed has tried to murder me and I'll fight fire with fire."

"You're wasting your breath," said Sally. "Can't you see that this man is as yellow as a canary?"

"What else can I do?" cried Sam Donnelly. "Go on, gunslinger. I'll pay you well."

Pete, dejected and not knowing what to do, turned and walked out of the room.

"I hope," said Sally, in scornful tones, "that Teed drills you, killer."

Pete went outside and looked at the vague shape of the buildings in the darkness. He had better get a little sleep and then try his luck at working this thing out. Meantime, Sally's tone rang spitefully in his ears. He had the feeling that she might do other than hate him. Perhaps . . .

Gunslinger? And he'd told his dad and promised himself that it was no trade to follow. Peace was the thing, and a man who didn't carry guns . . . Well, just this once. Just this once.

Chapter Five

PETE rolled out of his blankets while the world was still dark. He had not had more than an hour's sleep, but in that hour he had had so many nightmares that it was more blessed to stay awake and amidst the world's realities, however sad and trying they might be.

He saddled Ginger preparatory to leaving for town. He was convinced that he would have to follow the old man's orders, and he was certain that if he did he would lose Sally forever. He entertained hopes of what might happen afterwards, but he knew that they were impossible things and that Sally was not for him. She hated him and he would never be able to explain things to her. He was, in her eyes, that thing which he had tried so hard not to be, that thing which he had vowed to his dad that he would never be—a gunslinger.

He was about to return to the ranch house to borrow a Colt when he heard a faint thunder in the direction of Roundup. The sound came clearly on the crystal morning air. Hoofbeats!

His first impulse was to go to the house and then he realized that this was far from wise. If these were the vigilantes, and if he were caught again, no such miracle as had occurred before would save him.

He led Ginger down into a coulee and tied him loosely to some sage, then he returned and came closer to the house, remaining out of sight. He could hear Sally moving around in the kitchen.

A moment later a column of red-eyed and weary riders swung through the lower gate and stopped before the house, spraying dust before their hoofs.

Teed was on his black horse, flanked by the mountainous Rainy and the rail-thin Mungo. The vigilantes were riding again.

Teed bawled, "Come out of there!"

Sally came to the door. "What do you want?" She made it a casual question, but she stood very straight and her face was white.

"You know what we want!" roared the vigilantes. "Where's the Tornado?"

"He isn't here," said Sally.

"She's lying, boys," roared Teed. "You know what we found out. Sally Donnelly, you helped that gent escape last night. You was seen riding out of Roundup with him."

"You're sure of that?" said Sally, insolently.

"Not only of that," replied Teed with an ugly grin, "but sure that every penny of cash is gone from the bank. You and your dad helped him get away and in going you also robbed the bank."

"That's a lie!" cried Sally.

"Get Sam Donnelly," barked Teed.

Mungo and several others threw themselves off their horses and made for the house. Sally tried desperately to block their way, but they cast her back toward the horsemen and she was grabbed by the ready hands of Rainy who flung her across his horn.

From within the house came the sound of a struggle and Pete, out of sight, itched to put a couple shots where they would do the most good, but he had no gun and, besides, he thought he had a better plan.

Presently the vigilantes came back, dragging Sam Donnelly. The old man was pale and trembling, but he was mad all the way through and he gave them his best vocabulary.

In spite of the man's wounded condition, the vigilantes threw him across a saddle and tied him there.

"Scout around for that other gent," ordered Teed.

Pete hastily withdrew. There was certainly no point in getting caught by these fellows just now. Crawling backwards like a crab, Pete made his way back to Ginger.

After a few minutes' search the vigilantes mounted again and turned their horses toward town. From another coulee, Pete watched them go.

"The war," said Pete, "ain't begun, gents."

When the crowd had been gone a few minutes, Pete started out in their settling dust. He rode slowly as he had no wish to overtake them. He was bound for Roundup later in the day, but right now he had other things to worry about.

It seemed to him that the best course would be to find the Tornado and see what could be done in that quarter. He had no idea how the Tornado would treat him; in fact he did not spend much time worrying about it. The first thing to do would be to locate that elusive desperado and after that . . .

Two hours later Pete found the creek where he had met the man first. There had been neither wind nor rain since the meeting and it was fairly easy to pick out the tracks. Out of curiosity he backtracked himself and he found that the Tornado had also done this thing.

According to the hoofprints, the Tornado had found the gully and Pete's trail after he had left Sally and had then climbed up along the rim to follow Pete's course, finally coming down on the other side of the creek.

So far so good. Now, unless the man had left the country, Pete thought he stood some kind of a chance of connecting up with him again.

The trail he followed led north, into the buttes and coulees of a small range of hills. From time to time the Tornado had stopped and had examined his back trail to make certain that he was not being followed.

Once the Tornado had dismounted, and there beside his tracks Pete found an empty shell. Mounting again the man had ridden up to his kill, an antelope, had stripped away the best meat and had left the rest for the coyotes.

"There," said Pete. "He's sure to have built a fire unless he's Injun enough to eat it raw."

He did not think that the man would have gone far lugging that haunch of meat and so he left the tracks and made his way up to the hills without further inspection.

The morning air was lazy and it was possible to see for miles in any direction. In fact, when Pete mounted a crest he could look southeast to Roundup, a small huddle of unpainted shacks, lost in the immensity of the plains.

At last, after half an hour of careful observation, he found what he wanted, and what the Tornado must have tried hard to conceal. A plume of blue smoke was drifting straight up out of a canyon, like a thread connected to the sky.

Pete left Ginger and took the Tornado's riata, a sixty-foot rope, quite in keeping with the Spanish saddle. Loosening this as he went, walking gingerly over the rocks in his high-heeled boots, Pete came to a canyon rim and, throwing himself at full length, looked down.

Up against the wall, the Tornado was cooking breakfast, leaning low over his fire, turning a spitted roast of antelope. The aroma made Pete's mouth water and hardened his resolution to be fast and sure.

He eased a little closer and then, certain that he could not be seen from below while the Tornado still hung over his fire, he built his loop and cast it wooshing into the canyon.

It could not have been a neater throw. The wide loop dropped swiftly over the Tornado's head and Pete leaned back and took it in.

He pulled the Tornado off his feet and when the Tornado tried to go for his gun, Pete yanked again. Jerking the riata every third or fourth step, Pete went down the wall and came up to his captive.

"You!" snarled the man. "What's the idea?"

"Invitin' myself to breakfast," said Pete, deftly removing the Tornado's gun belts. Then he pressed the man down into the sand with one knee and began to tie him securely.

"You can't do this!" cried the man. "You . . . you ain't got any business . . ."

Pete ducked the man's head into the sand again and the Tornado, spitting grit, shut up. Quietly and thoroughly, Pete finished his task.

When the Tornado was comfortably seated up against the wall, Pete hunkered down beside the fire and the meat and calmly began turning it, just as though nothing at all had happened.

The Tornado did not wear a mask this morning and Pete studied the dark, stubbled face with interest. The Tornado had a lantern jaw and a broken nose and a livid scar which ran from his chin to his eye, splitting the side of his mouth.

"No wonder you wear that thing," said Pete. "How's your arm this morning?"

"You damned near kill me and then you ask how my arm is. *Phah!* Damn you, McClean. I'll drill you so full of holes you'll look like a gravel sifter."

"Maybe," said Pete. "But first you and I have got a job to do in Roundup. After that you can drill all you want to."

"Roundup! I can't go back there. They said I shot a guy and they'll hang me."

"Didn't you shoot him?"

"No, not on your life I didn't. I came into one end of town to look things over and a big thick guy—"

"That would be Rainy."

"And a big thick guy took a shot at me. And about a second later another shot sounded and a little gent in a dark suit fell down across the street. There wasn't nobody else in sight because it was too early."

"Then who did shoot Hastings, if you didn't?"

"S'help me, McClean, I wouldn't bother to lie out of a little thing like killin' a man. Come on and let me out of here."

"Not for a while," said Pete, stripping off antelope meat with the Tornado's knife. "Want some breakfast?"

Chapter Six

ROUNDUP, that night, was full of lights and laughter and gunshots. Occasionally outfits would ride in, yipping at the tops of their voices, and then make way for the first swinging door.

There would be, so the word had gone, a trial the next morning. And in the light of what had happened during that last trial, things ought to be interesting.

Out of respect for Sam Donnelly, in spite of the things the vigilantes had said he did, the town had insisted that he be put to bed in the hotel, and that Sally Donnelly be allowed to stay at the house of Widow Stephens, providing the house was heavily guarded.

The bank was the only quiet building there. It lay at the far end of the one street, a small fortlike chunk of granite, blending with the gloom.

No one noticed anything strange in the dark figure which stood there. The town was too full of men for one more to make any great difference. But any pair of eyes, probing deeper into that shadow, would have been amazed to see another man behind it, a man securely tied and gagged.

Pete was waiting for his chance. Much to his disgust, the bank was locked, but he could not have hoped that it would be otherwise. Now his only problem was to get into the bank.

In his hand he held one of the Tornado's pearl-handled six-guns, hefting it from time to time, restlessly.

If luck would favor him, everything would be fine.

Buzz Whitlaw, hobbling along on his Sharps, passed every now and then, very careful not to look into the shadow beside the bank. Whenever any citizen or puncher thought fit to pass that way, Buzz would swing in beside him and hold his attention by declaiming upon the subject of law and order and how the varmints ought to be hung to the nearest corral gate.

Pete had stood there for a long while. A coil of rope, his own, taken again from the Tornado, was beside him just in case he needed it.

Finally his prayers were answered, but in a startling way. He knew that any false move would discover him and that the cottonwood would be his immediate goal, trial or no trial. He had intended to somehow get Teed into the bank, alone.

But Teed, knowing that the Tornado was still loose, walked with both Rainy and Mungo flanking him.

The three came slowly up the street, evidently bent on entering the bank. Pete tensed. He knew he could not get the drop on all three at the same time.

Slowly he let out the riata and shook a loop.

Teed and his two henchmen came up to the door. Teed drew a ring of keys from his pocket and tried two of them to the locks.

Pete stepped into the street and motioned to Whitlaw and then, before the three had noticed his presence, Pete built a swift loop, gauged his distance and threw.

A startled yelp from the group was immediately followed by a thud. As though he bulldogged a steer, Pete leaned back and brought them crashing to the ground in a helpless pile. Buzz Whitlaw hobbled up, his Sharps ready. Pete knelt over the floundering pile and began to whisk away their guns.

"Damn you!" screamed Teed. "I'll—"

"Shut up," said Buzz, hoarsely. "Or we'll drill you right now."

The town was too busy drinking to notice what had gone on in the shadows before the bank, and with the rope still cutting the ribs of his captives, Pete successfully herded them into the interior, Buzz Whitlaw following.

But when they reached those close confines and when the three realized that they were faced by only one man and a cripple, they decided with one accord that they were the better men.

Rainy threw out his great arms and shook the rope open. He dived out of the loop, rightly guessing that Pete would not fire.

The move was so sudden that Pete's attention was momentarily withdrawn from Teed. Teed dived at his desk and clawed at the top drawer. Mungo went the other way toward a rifle rack.

Three men going in different directions in the space of a second offer very bad targets for one six-gun. Pete did not bother, and he did not dare fire and alarm the town.

With an expert flip, Pete drove the butt down on Teed's fingers. Pete whirled and brought the pearl handle up into Rainy's jaw. Then he whirled and knocked Teed down again.

Pete whipped about, expecting to be set upon from the

rear by Mungo, but Mungo's thin length was measuring the rug and Buzz Whitlaw was leaning upon his Sharps, ready to take the situation over.

"They're out," commented Buzz. "Reckon you better put hobbles on 'em, son."

Pete tied the toppling Teed into his desk chair, fastening his ankles to the chair legs and leaving his arms free. Then, in like fashion, he secured both Rainy and Mungo so that it appeared that they merely sat with their legs under them.

He placed these two men on either side of the desk and stood back to admire them, although he could see very little by the light which came in through the window.

"Don't they look natural?" said Buzz.

"They'll wake up after a while, I hope," said Pete. "Now for the Tornado."

"But I thought," said Buzz, "I thought you was . . ."

Pete was already gone. He came back in a minute carrying his man. Approaching the grated vault, Pete cast the raving desperado inside and loosened up his bonds so that he could climb out of them with a moment's work. Then Pete went out of the vault and closed and locked the brass grate.

The Tornado could see the rest of the room very well but he was in the dark.

"Now," said Pete, "are you willing to listen to reason?"

"Let me out of here, damn it."

"No. Not right now. You're there and you'll stay there until I let you out. It won't do you any good to try to kill me because that would fix you right up. Your wounded arm marks you."

"But what the hell is the big idea?"

Pete shook his head. "If you've got sense, mister, you'll let me handle this. There's bigger things than my life or yours at stake and if you'll promise to be good and not try to use it on me, I'll slip you one of your guns."

"You will? All right, I promise."

Pete grinned and passed the six-gun through the grate. "There you are. That's something anyhow. But don't get funny and try to nail me or make me open up, because you could hand me all six slugs and I wouldn't."

Very puzzled, the Tornado subsided and melted back into the darkness of the vault.

Pete went to the desk. Teed glared at him from bloodshot eyes and nursed his mashed fingers.

"I want," said Pete, "to look through your personal papers."

"No! Get away from here!"

Mungo lifted his head and stared at them for some while. He did not seem to be so very interested. Rainy was still out. They all bore the scars of the battle.

Pete flipped open the drawers, one after another, looking for something which looked like a personal record. He knew that Teed would have to keep one of some kind.

Finally, in a small black book, he saw initials and numbers without dollar marks.

"T—one thousand. R—five hundred. A.N.—six hundred." Pete stopped reading and looked puzzled. He turned other pages and read things there and then shoved the book into his hip pocket.

"Gentlemen," said Pete, now that Rainy had revived, "I would be very careful of what I did. Behind you in that vault

I've got a man-eating cougar who would appreciate a chance to shoot you down. And he will because he doesn't like any of you."

"What's this all about?" demanded Teed.

"Buzz," said Pete. "You go tell the six leadin' citizens who are directors and financiers of this bank, that there's a meeting called right away. And don't be too long about it."

"I get it," said Buzz. He grinned and stumped away upon his trusty Sharps.

Chapter Seven

PETE arranged his stage to suit him. He lit all the lamps he could find and placed them in their wall brackets. He placed a half-dozen chairs along the wall for the directors and found a box of cigars which he placed beside a whiskey bottle on the table. Through it all he was eyed malignantly by his three captives, and from time to time, muttered remarks none too complimentary came from the vault.

Then Pete retired into the gloomy shadows outside and waited. Presently Buzz Whitlaw, followed by several men, came up and entered the bank, and a little later others came. They were all frock-coated, substantial citizens, looking respectable and peaceful and well fed, although their chests bulged with holstered revolvers habitually carried.

When they were all inside, Pete heard chairs scrape. He did not hear either Teed or his henchmen say a word.

The time had come for the entrance of Pete. Juggling the pearl-handled gun, he went in.

Except for Teed, the others had their backs to him. Buzz was on the lookout and the instant Pete appeared, the Sharps swung up to control the situation.

"Keep your seats, gentlemen," said Pete, amiably. "I called this meeting."

The men swiveled around, astonishment quickly masked

upon their hard faces. But they were mindful of the Sharps on one side and the Colt on the other and they knew a trap when they saw it.

"What's the meaning of this?" thundered Hanson, a big, white-whiskered man.

"You're going to have a meeting," said Pete, "and if you think you can do anything about it, look at the grate over there."

They looked but all they could see was a hand and a Colt. It was enough.

"Now," said Pete, "you thought you were going to have a trial in the morning. I think you're going to have a trial right now. The guilty men—or rather the defendants—are your pals Teed and Rainy and Mungo. Don't bother about them, they're tame as kittens and they're tied, whether it looks like it or not."

"Is this true?" bellowed Hanson at Teed.

Teed merely glared.

"Look here," said a small, thin fellow with a blotchy face, "you kept us here all morning, Teed, checking up on the cash that was stolen. Is this another game of yours?"

"Another game," said Pete. "I'm going to show you gentlemen some things you don't know about banking. You all have an interest in this, I suppose."

"Thirty thousand apiece," said Hanson.

"Then—" began Pete, but he never finished the sentence. A soft footfall sounded behind him.

"Reach for the ceiling," rasped a man behind Pete.

Buzz raised the Sharps again and then saw that the window and the door were filled to overflowing with guns.

Pete turned slowly, lowering his Colt, and discovered that the man behind him was another member of the vigilantes.

"We got the word," said the vigilante, "and we came runnin'. Don't try nothin', Tornado. We're plenty ready for you."

The men in the doorway moved aside and Sally was thrust into the room. She came unwillingly and when she saw Pete, a fleeting expression passed through her eyes which made Pete's heart leap. But the glance turned cold in the same instant.

"We thought you might need her," said the vigilante, "and so we brung her along."

Hanson stood up with a slow smile. "Have a seat, mister."

Pete sat down.

Teed reared up in sudden hope. "Now you've got the killer again. Now we can string him up. Come on, boys. We don't need any trial now."

"Wait a minute," said Hanson. "Dead men can't talk and this gent wouldn't have come here if he didn't have something to say to us."

"He's full of lies!" yelled Teed.

"He's framin' us," barked Mungo.

Hanson turned to Pete. "As far as you're concerned, mister, you're just a gunfighter with a fancy handle and we'd rather kill you than not. But if you've got anything to say—"

"I've got plenty to say," said Pete, coolly. "I've got a book here . . . and I'm going after a book, not a gun, boys." He took the black leaflet from his pocket and opened it on the table.

"In there," said Pete, "you'll find that Teed has listed bribes under initials. Name your punchers that left you, Miss Sally."

Sally frowned a little and then said, "Randolph and Andy Newton and Bart Townsend and—"

"That's enough," said Pete. "Look at this book. Here's R—five hundred, T—one thousand, and A.N.—six hundred and so on. That's Teed's book and that's Teed's writing. Why did these boys leave you, Miss Sally?"

"I—I don't know. They went away and I heard that they said they quit because they wouldn't work for a crooked outfit."

"They were bribed with these amounts," said Pete.

A sudden commotion appeared in the doorway and a man was catapulted into the room. He averted his eyes from Sally, and Pete recognized him to be the one who had thrown the rope the day before.

"Is that true, Randolph?" cried Hanson.

Randolph hung his head and then, finding that he was the target, finally nodded that it was.

"There you are," said Pete. "Teed bribed these men with a promise of land and that money and they left. Teed was trying to shake Donnelly out of the Golden Valley ranch. He couldn't loan Donnelly money so he tried to run Donnelly out of the country. My idea is that Teed was trying to get hold of that land in a slick way, seeing that it got sold off. He would back the mortgages of the small owners and then he'd have control of the finest land around here, through the bank, and nothing would ever trace itself back to him."

"By God," said Hanson, "I thought it looked funny. What about this robbery?"

"Teed couldn't account for those sums and so, when I escaped last night, he said I had stolen them."

"So that's how you used the vigilantes," roared the man behind Pete. "Here, let this Tornado loose. He—"

Teed, up until now, had remained impassive, but suddenly he yelled, "That don't excuse him for murderin' Hastings, my cashier!"

The directors and the faces at the door and window turned again to Pete.

Pete looked at Sally. "Miss Sally, how did this Tornado come to you?"

"He came . . . I don't know," said Sally. "Dad never sent for him."

"There you are," said Pete. "The Tornado was hired by—"

"Wait a minute," said Hanson. "*You're* the Tornado."

"The hell I am," said Pete. "Listen. Teed imported the Tornado, then had Mungo shoot Hastings, who knew too much, and blamed it on the gunman. Teed thought he could tangle up Donnelly by putting his own man in Donnelly's employ."

Pete stared at the grate. "And that was why the Tornado was imported."

"Then Teed—" began Hanson.

"Look out!" screamed Sally.

Pete had forgotten one thing. The gun in the upper drawer. Under the cover of the desk, Teed had it.

Pete dived sideways. The gun crashed and sent Pete spinning. Another report blasted through the room and smoke leaped out from the grate. Teed fell.

Mungo lurched forward and snatched at Hanson's shoulder gun. The vigilante fired and Mungo flattened out and dived inert under the desk, banging the chair down on top of himself. Rainy sat very still and said nothing.

An eddying coil of blue smoke drifted through the room, hanging like a shroud over the hushed men.

Pete turned a little and groaned, trying to sit up. Hanson started to kneel but Sally was there first, lifting Pete's head.

"Just . . . just tagged me . . . in the side," said Pete. "Be . . . all right . . . when I get my . . . my breath."

Hanson turned on Rainy. "Then what about this? Is this man the Tornado or not?"

"Hell, no!" bellowed the man in the vault. "Let me out of here."

They let him out. He had again covered his face with a mask and he stood looking down at Teed. "The double-crossing son of a gun. Settin' his own men on me and then lightin' out after me with a posse just like he never hired me at all."

Hanson stood back and the Tornado did not seem to be aware of the guns which covered him. He turned and looked at the faces about him. "That kid is Tad McClean's boy and he ain't no gunslinger. As for this Rainy, he plugged me and you'd better hoist him high. And as for me, gentlemen, havin' done my good deed by killin' this lobo Teed, I'll be on my way."

They did not stop him as he went out. They were too thunderstruck by his utter indifference to them, too impressed by the gun in his hand. He stopped at the door and looked at Pete, who was miraculously revived in Sally's arms.

"As for you, kid, I guess you was right. Guns never did nobody any good."

He was gone and they heard Ginger's hoofs clattering as he rode away.

"Hell," said Hanson, "you can't hang a public benefactor like that."

Two men came carrying the raging Sam Donnelly between them and Sam was properly silenced while affairs were explained to him. It took him quite a while to get things straight and then he roared, "By God, I'll make him my foreman. Damned if not."

"Foreman," said Hanson. "Foreman! He's going to be Roundup's marshal, that's what!"

"I said foreman!" bellowed Sam.

"Marshal!" thundered Hanson.

Pete, on the floor, looked up at Sally and said, "Gee, I didn't think you were ever going to smile at me."

Story Preview

Story Preview

NOW that you've just ventured through some of the captivating tales in the Stories from the Golden Age collection by L. Ron Hubbard, turn the page and enjoy a preview of *The No-Gun Man*. Join Monte Calhoun as he returns home to the town of Superstition only to find his father murdered in an underhanded attempt to steal his gold mining claims. When the entire town demands he avenge his father, it triggers a conflict within Monte that's both unexpected and fateful.

The No-Gun Man

"MY dear fellow," said O'Leary, "this is the tenth time you've alluded to this. I am afraid I don't understand. Calhoun seems a very nice fellow. I couldn't possibly connect him with murder."

Old Darby laughed gleefully. "Maybe not, Captain. Maybe not. But you just wait until we get to Superstition; you'll whistle another tune. They up and done what they done and now they got to take their consequences. Yessirree. Take their consequences and get buried."

"Who?" demanded O'Leary.

"Why, old Spiegel and his condemned boys, that's who!"

O'Leary sighed. "And what does this Spiegel have to do with Monte Calhoun?"

"Why, they just killed his father, that's all. Oh, you wait! There'll be powder smoke until you can't breathe for it! You just wait!"

"You mean somebody is going to try to kill Calhoun?"

"No, no! T'other way around. Monte, he's a sly one. He ain't lettin' on." And Darby slapped the captain's back, did another dance step and jumped up to the box.

O'Leary got in and looked wonderingly at Monte. That person had now consigned himself to slumber and in sleep he

113

looked very angelic and not at all murderous. The starting of
the coach wakened him and he sat up so that O'Leary could
sit down.

The captain was silent for some miles and then, in
consideration of his official position, decided to brave it. He
had taken a fancy to young Monte.

"Did you ever hear," said O'Leary, "of a man named
Spiegel?"

Monte looked at him, pushed back his hat with his thumb
and cocked his head over on one side, questioningly. "He
owns the Diamond Queen. Sure."

The captain felt that he was on delicate ground. "Did
you . . . er . . . have you . . . well, that is to say . . . Are you
planning to kill him?"

Monte blinked. "Kill Spiegel?"

The captain shrugged. "Well, if you don't want to confide
in me . . ." He was disappointed. During this long ride from
the East he had decided that Monte Calhoun was a friend
he would like to have and keep. The young man's unfailing
humor, his calm presence and his good sense loomed large
in the captain's mind.

Monte pulled his hat back down. He was frowning in
thought. Suddenly he snapped his fingers. "So *that's* what
Old Darby has been caterwauling about! Oh, my gosh!" He
looked for a moment as if he would crawl out and up to the
box and give Darby a piece of his mind and then relaxed. "So
that's what they've figured!"

O'Leary respected the pause, for he knew Monte would
go on.

The young man settled himself and looked at the captain. "Terence, I'd forgotten that the territorial government had asked you to go to Superstition and declare war on the lawless. You're interested and you've got an explanation coming, but if you think I am going to kill anybody, you're wrong."

The captain looked relieved but still a trifle doubtful.

"Terence, four years ago this might have been the case. But I hope that the time I spent studying mining engineering also taught me some sense. Last year my father was murdered by a person or persons unknown. I am afraid that this did not make a very deep impression on me.

"When I was very small, my mother and I were dragged West and hauled through various gold rushes and stampedes, one boomtown and then another, living on canned beans and drinking alkali water. The old man was a pretty tough fellow. He took what he wanted and he never showed anybody much mercy. Particularly my mother. He knew she was sick and yet he dragged her around with him until she finally died. I was just a little kid but I remember it well enough.

"He struck it rich the following year. Found the Deserter Lode on the east side of that range up ahead and sat himself down to gouge every nickel out of it that he could. *Peón* labor and bullets for anybody who would contest his desires. He was a tough man.

"I went to school and got out of it, learned to eat with a fork and travel a hundred yards without forking a horse. I found out there was something in life besides hating and grabbing.

"Last year my father was ambushed and murdered. Nobody

ever identified the bushwhackers. The thing came to trial before Judge Talbot of the territorial government, and this man Spiegel and his three sons were freed of any suspicion. Nobody ever found who killed my father.

"I've got a kid brother, Dick, about sixteen or seventeen now. He's been out here all this time, growing up like sagebrush. I've come out to sell the mine and take Dick back to civilization before he's past salvaging."

He fell silent and then, after a little, said, "So they think *that's* why I'm coming back."

"You must have enjoyed a reputation out here once for them to think that," said O'Leary.

"Perhaps. Oh, sure. When I was a little younger I thought the thing to do was drink hard and shoot straight and beat yourself on the chest to the men who drank your whiskey. But you can forget about any trouble you might have with me, Terence. I've got no intention of opening the play on a man the law has already absolved from guilt."

O'Leary sat silent, thinking about this. And then he muttered, "Maybe not now, my boy. But they've got their codes out here. It isn't so much what you'll do. What are *they* going to do?"

"What?" said Monte.

"Nothing," said O'Leary. "Just looking at that range of hills over there. Pretty, huh? Like a row of tombstones!"

To find out more about *The No-Gun Man* and how you can obtain your copy, go to www.goldenagestories.com.

Glossary

Glossary

STORIES FROM THE GOLDEN AGE *reflect the words and expressions used in the 1930s and 1940s, adding unique flavor and authenticity to the tales. While a character's speech may often reflect regional origins, it also can convey attitudes common in the day. So that readers can better grasp such cultural and historical terms, uncommon words or expressions of the era, the following glossary has been provided.*

alkali: a powdery white mineral that salts the ground in many low places in the West. It whitens the ground where water has risen to the surface and gone back down.

ambuscaderos: officers of the law who ambush people. This is a coined word from *am*bush and *buscadero,* a word meaning a tough, gun-packing officer of the law.

batwings: long chaps (leather leggings the cowboy wears to protect his legs) with big flaps of leather. They usually fasten with rings and snaps.

Bird Cage Opera House: a combination saloon, gambling hall and brothel. The name was a fancy way in the 1880s of describing such a place.

blamed: confounded.

boomtown: a community that experiences sudden and rapid population and economic growth, normally attributed to the nearby discovery of gold, silver or oil. The gold rush of the American Southwest is the most famous example, as towns would seemingly sprout up from the desert around what was thought to be valuable gold mining country.

Boot Hill: a cemetery in a settlement on the US frontier, especially one for gunfighters killed in action. It was given its name because most of its early occupants died with their boots on.

box: the stagecoach driver's seat.

bulldog: to throw a calf or steer by seizing the horns and twisting its neck until the animal loses its balance and falls.

cantle: the raised back part of a saddle for a horse.

caterwauling: making a harsh, disagreeable noise that sounds like the cry of cats.

chinkies: chinks; short leather chaps (leggings), usually fringed and stopping just below the knee, worn over the pants for protection.

clapboard: a type of siding covering the outer walls of buildings in which one edge of each long thin board is thicker than the other. The thick edge of each board overlaps the thin edge of the board below it.

Colt: a single-action, six-shot cylinder revolver, most commonly available in .45- or .44-caliber versions. It was first manufactured in 1873 for the Army by the Colt Firearms Company, the armory founded by American inventor Samuel Colt (1814–1862) who revolutionized the firearms industry with the invention of the revolver. The Colt, also known as the Peacemaker, was also made available to civilians. As a reliable, inexpensive and popular handgun among cowboys, it became known as the "cowboy's gun" and a symbol of the Old West.

concha: a disk, traditionally of hammered silver and resembling a shell or flower, used as a decoration piece on belts, harnesses, etc.

cordon sanitaire: (French) a barrier designed to prevent undesirable conditions from spreading.

cottonwood: hanging tree; the trademark tree of the West, growing along the banks of rivers and creeks, which was commonly used for lynchings. A man lynched from the limb of a tree was referred to as a *cottonwood blossom.*

coulee: a deep ravine or gulch, usually dry, that has been formed by running water.

cow town: a town at the end of the trail from which cattle were shipped; later applied to towns in the cattle country that depended upon the cowman and his trade for their existence.

coyote: used for a man who has the sneaking and skulking characteristics of a coyote.

dernier ressort: (French) last resort.

devils of the air: spirits who hover around the earth.

Dieu défend le droit: (French) God defends the right.

doggone: damned.

faro: a gambling game played with cards and popular in the American West of the nineteenth century. In faro, the players bet on the order in which the cards will be turned over by the dealer. The cards were kept in a dealing box to keep track of the play.

foofaraw: an excessive amount of decoration or ornamentation.

forking: mounting (a horse).

G-men: government men; agents of the Federal Bureau of Investigation.

gunhawk: a wandering gunfighter.

hawg laig: hog leg; another name for the popular Colt revolver also known as the Peacemaker.

hayrick or **rick:** a large stack or pile of hay, straw, corn or the like, especially when thatched or covered by a tarp.

Henry: the first rifle to use a cartridge with a metallic casing rather than the undependable, self-contained powder, ball and primer of previous rifles. It was named after B. Tyler Henry, who designed the rifle and the cartridge.

hobbles: (usually attributed to horses) short lengths of rope used to fasten the legs together to prevent free motion.

Holliday, Doc: John Henry Holliday (1851–1887), an American dentist, gambler and gunfighter of the Old West frontier. He is usually remembered for his association with the famous marshal of the Arizona Territory, Wyatt Earp, whom he joined in the famous gunfight at the OK Corral against members of the Clanton gang of suspected cattle rustlers.

honi soit qui mal y pense: (French) evil to him who thinks evil of it.

iron: a handgun, especially a revolver.

John B.: Stetson.

Judge Colt: nickname for the single-action (that is, cocked by hand for each shot), six-shot Army model revolver first produced in 1873 by Colt Firearms Company, the armory founded by Samuel Colt (1814–1862). The handgun of the Old West became the instrument of both lawmaker and lawbreaker during the last twenty-five years of the nineteenth century. It soon earned various names, such as "Peacemaker," "Equalizer" and "Judge Colt and his jury of six."

kingpin: the most important person in a group or undertaking.

lantern jaw: a distinctly protruding, often wide lower jaw.

lex scripta: (Latin) written law.

lex talionis: (Latin) the legal principle that prescribes retaliating in kind for crimes committed.

light out or **lit out:** to leave quickly; depart hurriedly.

Limited: a train line making only a limited number of stops en route. The full name for the line was often abbreviated down to simply *Limited.*

lobo: wolf; one who is regarded as predatory, greedy and fierce.

lode: a deposit of ore that fills a fissure in a rock, or a vein of ore deposited between layers of rock.

lynch mob: a group of people who capture and hang someone without legal arrest and trial, because they think the person has committed a crime.

macheer: a type of saddle with a *mochila* (Spanish for *knapsack*), a covering of leather that fits over the top of the saddle. Attached to the *mochila* were four boxes of hard leather used for transport of letters. The design allowed for easy and quick removal and placement on a fresh horse at remount stations, or if the horse were killed, the rider could strip the *mochila* and walk to the next station.

Masterson: William Barclay "Bat" Masterson (1853–1921), a legendary figure of the American West. He lived an adventurous life, which included stints as a buffalo hunter, US Army scout, gambler, frontier lawman, US marshal and, finally, sports editor and columnist for a New York newspaper.

mesquite: any of several small spiny trees or shrubs native to the southwestern US and Mexico, and important as plants for bees and forage for cattle.

neck-reined: guided a horse by pressure of the reins against its neck.

pegged: threw.

peón: (Spanish) a farm worker or unskilled laborer; day laborer.

prickly pear: a cactus with flattened, jointed, spiny stems and pear-shaped fruits that are edible in some species.

proddy: inclined to prod or goad to action; tending to incite.

puncher: a hired hand who tends cattle and performs other duties on horseback.

quirt: a riding whip with a short handle and a braided leather lash.

rannies: ranahans; cowboys or top ranch hands.

repeater watch: a pocket watch that chimes every one, twelve or twenty-four hours.

revenons à nos moutons: (French) let us return to our sheep.

riata: a long noosed rope used to catch animals.

Roman holiday: a violent public spectacle or disturbance in which shame, degradation or physical harm is intentionally inflicted on one person or group by another or others. It comes from the bloody gladiatorial contests staged as entertainment for the ancient Romans.

Scheherazade: the female narrator of *The Arabian Nights,* who during one thousand and one adventurous nights saved her life by entertaining her husband, the king, with stories.

Seco Hombre: (Spanish) dry man. Used here as the name of a saloon.

section hand: tracklayer; a workman who lays and repairs railroad tracks.

Sharps: any of several models of firearms devised by Christian Sharps and produced by the Sharps Rifle Company until 1881. The most popular Sharps were "Old Reliable," the cavalry carbine, and the heavy-caliber, single-shot buffalo-hunting rifle. Because of its low muzzle velocity, this gun was said to "fire today, kill tomorrow."

Sic semper tyrannis: (Latin) Thus always to tyrants.

sidewinder: rattlesnake.

Stetson: as the most popular broad-brimmed hat in the West, it became the generic name for *hat*. John B. Stetson was a master hat maker and founder of the company that has been making Stetsons since 1865. Not only can the Stetson stand up to a terrific amount of beating, the cowboy's hat has more different uses than any other garment he wears. It keeps the sun out of the eyes and off the neck; it serves as an umbrella; it makes a great fan, which sometimes is needed when building a fire or shunting cattle about; the brim serves as a cup to water oneself, or as a bucket to water the horse or put out the fire.

tenpins: rounded, bottle-shaped wooden clubs used in a bowling game, which go flying when hit.

Thompson, Ben: (1842–1884) a gunman, gambler and sometime lawman of the American Old West. He was a private in the Confederate States Army during the American Civil War and subsequently fought in Mexico before being imprisoned for murder. After his release from prison, he made his name as a gunman and a gambler before being offered the job as marshal in Austin, Texas, during which time the crime rate fell dramatically.

varmints: those people who are obnoxious or make trouble.

vi et armis: (Latin) by force of arms.

vigilantes: citizens banded together in the West as vigilance committees, without legal sanction and usually in the absence of effective law enforcement, to take action against men viewed as threats to life and property. The usual pattern of vigilance committees was to grab their enemies (guilty or not), stage a sort of trial and hang them. Their other enemies were then likely to get out of town.

war sack: a cowboy's bag for his personal possessions, plunder, cartridges, etc. Often made of canvas but sometimes just a flour or grain sack, it is usually tied behind the saddle.

whistling post: whistle stop; a small town or community.

Wild Bill Hickok: (1837–1876) a legendary figure in the American Old West. After fighting in the Union Army during the US Civil War, he became a famous Army scout and later a lawman and gunfighter.

Winchester: an early family of repeating rifles; a single-barreled rifle containing multiple rounds of ammunition. Manufactured by the Winchester Repeating Arms Company, it was widely used in the US during the latter half of the nineteenth century. The 1873 model is often called "the gun that won the West" for its immense popularity at that time, as well as its use in fictional Westerns.

wind devils: spinning columns of air that move across the landscape and pick up loose dust. They look like miniature tornados, but are not as powerful.

ye: you.

L. Ron Hubbard
in the Golden Age
of Pulp Fiction

*In writing an adventure story
a writer has to know that he is adventuring
for a lot of people who cannot.
The writer has to take them here and there
about the globe and show them
excitement and love and realism.
As long as that writer is living the part of an
adventurer when he is hammering
the keys, he is succeeding with his story.*

*Adventuring is a state of mind.
If you adventure through life, you have a
good chance to be a success on paper.*

*Adventure doesn't mean globe-trotting,
exactly, and it doesn't mean great deeds.
Adventuring is like art.
You have to live it to make it real.*

— *L. RON HUBBARD*

L. Ron Hubbard
and American
Pulp Fiction

Born March 13, 1911, L. Ron Hubbard lived a life at least as expansive as the stories with which he enthralled a hundred million readers through a fifty-year career.

Originally hailing from Tilden, Nebraska, he spent his formative years in a classically rugged Montana, replete with the cowpunchers, lawmen and desperadoes who would later people his Wild West adventures. And lest anyone imagine those adventures were drawn from vicarious experience, he was not only breaking broncs at a tender age, he was also among the few whites ever admitted into Blackfoot society as a bona fide blood brother. While if only to round out an otherwise rough and tumble youth, his mother was that rarity of her time—a thoroughly educated woman—who introduced her son to the classics of Occidental literature even before his seventh birthday.

But as any dedicated L. Ron Hubbard reader will attest, his world extended far beyond Montana. In point of fact, and as the son of a United States naval officer, by the age of eighteen he had traveled over a quarter of a million miles. Included therein were three Pacific crossings to a then still mysterious Asia, where he ran with the likes of Her British Majesty's agent-in-place

L. Ron Hubbard, left, at Congressional Airport, Washington, DC, 1931, with members of George Washington University flying club.

for North China, and the last in the line of Royal Magicians from the court of Kublai Khan. For the record, L. Ron Hubbard was also among the first Westerners to gain admittance to forbidden Tibetan monasteries below Manchuria, and his photographs of China's Great Wall long graced American geography texts.

Upon his return to the United States and a hasty completion of his interrupted high school education, the young Ron Hubbard entered George Washington University. There, as fans of his aerial adventures may have heard, he earned his wings as a pioneering barnstormer at the dawn of American aviation. He also earned a place in free-flight record books for the longest sustained flight above Chicago. Moreover, as a roving reporter for *Sportsman Pilot* (featuring his first professionally penned articles), he further helped inspire a generation of pilots who would take America to world airpower.

Immediately beyond his sophomore year, Ron embarked on the first of his famed ethnological expeditions, initially to then untrammeled Caribbean shores (descriptions of which would later fill a whole series of West Indies mystery-thrillers). That the Puerto Rican interior would also figure into the future of Ron Hubbard stories was likewise no accident. For in addition to cultural studies of the island, a 1932–33

LRH expedition is rightly remembered as conducting the first complete mineralogical survey of a Puerto Rico under United States jurisdiction.

There was many another adventure along this vein: As a lifetime member of the famed Explorers Club, L. Ron Hubbard charted North Pacific waters with the first shipboard radio direction finder, and so pioneered a long-range navigation system universally employed until the late twentieth century. While not to put too fine an edge on it, he also held a rare Master Mariner's license to pilot any vessel, of any tonnage in any ocean.

Yet lest we stray too far afield, there is an LRH note at this juncture in his saga, and it reads in part:

"I started out writing for the pulps, writing the best I knew, writing for every mag on the stands, slanting as well as I could."

Capt. L. Ron Hubbard in Ketchikan, Alaska, 1940, on his Alaskan Radio Experimental Expedition, the first of three voyages conducted under the Explorers Club flag.

To which one might add: His earliest submissions date from the summer of 1934, and included tales drawn from true-to-life Asian adventures, with characters roughly modeled on British/American intelligence operatives he had known in Shanghai. His early Westerns were similarly peppered with details drawn from personal experience. Although therein lay a first hard lesson from the often cruel world of the pulps. His first Westerns were soundly rejected as lacking the authenticity of a Max Brand yarn (a particularly frustrating comment given L. Ron Hubbard's Westerns came straight from his Montana homeland, while Max Brand was a mediocre New York poet named Frederick Schiller Faust, who turned out implausible six-shooter tales from the terrace of an Italian villa).

Nevertheless, and needless to say, L. Ron Hubbard persevered and soon earned a reputation as among the most publishable names in pulp fiction, with a ninety percent placement rate of first-draft manuscripts. He was also among the most prolific, averaging between seventy and a hundred thousand words a month. Hence the rumors that L. Ron Hubbard had redesigned a typewriter for faster keyboard action and pounded out manuscripts on a continuous roll of butcher paper to save the precious seconds it took to insert a single sheet of paper into manual typewriters of the day.

That all L. Ron Hubbard stories did not run beneath said byline is yet another aspect of pulp fiction lore. That is, as publishers periodically rejected manuscripts from top-drawer authors if only to avoid paying top dollar, L. Ron Hubbard and company just as frequently replied with submissions under various pseudonyms. In Ron's case, the list

A MAN OF MANY NAMES

Between 1934 and 1950, L. Ron Hubbard authored more than fifteen million words of fiction in more than two hundred classic publications. To supply his fans and editors with stories across an array of genres and pulp titles, he adopted fifteen pseudonyms in addition to his already renowned L. Ron Hubbard byline.

Winchester Remington Colt
Lt. Jonathan Daly
Capt. Charles Gordon
Capt. L. Ron Hubbard
Bernard Hubbel
Michael Keith
Rene Lafayette
Legionnaire 148
Legionnaire 14830
Ken Martin
Scott Morgan
Lt. Scott Morgan
Kurt von Rachen
Barry Randolph
Capt. Humbert Reynolds

included: Rene Lafayette, Captain Charles Gordon, Lt. Scott Morgan and the notorious Kurt von Rachen—supposedly on the lam for a murder rap, while hammering out two-fisted prose in Argentina. The point: While L. Ron Hubbard as Ken Martin spun stories of Southeast Asian intrigue, LRH as Barry Randolph authored tales of romance on the Western range—which, stretching between a dozen genres is how he came to stand among the two hundred elite authors providing close to a million tales through the glory days of American Pulp Fiction.

L. Ron Hubbard, circa 1930, at the outset of a literary career that would finally span half a century.

In evidence of exactly that, by 1936 L. Ron Hubbard was literally leading pulp fiction's elite as president of New York's American Fiction Guild. Members included a veritable pulp hall of fame: Lester "Doc Savage" Dent, Walter "The Shadow" Gibson, and the legendary Dashiell Hammett—to cite but a few.

Also in evidence of just where L. Ron Hubbard stood within his first two years on the American pulp circuit: By the spring of 1937, he was ensconced in Hollywood, adopting a Caribbean thriller for Columbia Pictures, remembered today as *The Secret of Treasure Island.* Comprising fifteen thirty-minute episodes, the L. Ron Hubbard screenplay led to the most profitable matinée serial in Hollywood history. In accord with Hollywood culture, he was thereafter continually called

135

The 1937 Secret of Treasure Island, *a fifteen-episode serial adapted for the screen by L. Ron Hubbard from his novel,* Murder at Pirate Castle.

upon to rewrite/doctor scripts—most famously for long-time friend and fellow adventurer Clark Gable.

In the interim—and herein lies another distinctive chapter of the L. Ron Hubbard story—he continually worked to open Pulp Kingdom gates to up-and-coming authors. Or, for that matter, anyone who wished to write. It was a fairly unconventional stance, as markets were already thin and competition razor sharp. But the fact remains, it was an L. Ron Hubbard hallmark that he vehemently lobbied on behalf of young authors—regularly supplying instructional articles to trade journals, guest-lecturing to short story classes at George Washington University and Harvard, and even founding his own creative writing competition. It was established in 1940, dubbed the Golden Pen, and guaranteed winners both New York representation and publication in *Argosy*.

But it was John W. Campbell Jr.'s *Astounding Science Fiction* that finally proved the most memorable LRH vehicle. While every fan of L. Ron Hubbard's galactic epics undoubtedly knows the story, it nonetheless bears repeating: By late 1938, the pulp publishing magnate of Street & Smith was determined to revamp *Astounding Science Fiction* for broader readership. In particular, senior editorial director F. Orlin Tremaine called for stories with a stronger *human element*. When acting editor John W. Campbell balked, preferring his spaceship-driven tales,

136

Tremaine enlisted Hubbard. Hubbard, in turn, replied with the genre's first truly *character-driven* works, wherein heroes are pitted not against bug-eyed monsters but the mystery and majesty of deep space itself—and thus was launched the Golden Age of Science Fiction.

The names alone are enough to quicken the pulse of any science fiction aficionado, including LRH friend and protégé, Robert Heinlein, Isaac Asimov, A. E. van Vogt and Ray Bradbury. Moreover, when coupled with LRH stories of fantasy, we further come to what's rightly been described as the foundation of every modern tale of horror: L. Ron Hubbard's immortal *Fear.* It was rightly proclaimed by Stephen King as one of the very few works to genuinely warrant that overworked term "classic"—as in: *"This is a classic tale of creeping, surreal menace and horror. . . . This is one of the really, really good ones."*

L. Ron Hubbard, 1948, among fellow science fiction luminaries at the World Science Fiction Convention in Toronto.

To accommodate the greater body of L. Ron Hubbard fantasies, Street & Smith inaugurated *Unknown*—a classic pulp if there ever was one, and wherein readers were soon thrilling to the likes of *Typewriter in the Sky* and *Slaves of Sleep* of which Frederik Pohl would declare: *"There are bits and pieces from Ron's work that became part of the language in ways that very few other writers managed."*

And, indeed, at J. W. Campbell Jr.'s insistence, Ron was regularly drawing on themes from the Arabian Nights and

137

so introducing readers to a world of genies, jinn, Aladdin and Sinbad—all of which, of course, continue to float through cultural mythology to this day.

At least as influential in terms of post-apocalypse stories was L. Ron Hubbard's 1940 *Final Blackout*. Generally acclaimed as the finest anti-war novel of the decade and among the ten best works of the genre ever authored—here, too, was a tale that would live on in ways few other writers

imagined. Hence, the later Robert Heinlein verdict: "Final Blackout *is as perfect a piece of science fiction as has ever been written.*"

Like many another who both lived and wrote American pulp adventure, the war proved a tragic end to Ron's sojourn in the pulps. He served with distinction in four theaters and was highly decorated

Portland, Oregon, 1943; L. Ron Hubbard captain of the US Navy subchaser PC 815.

for commanding corvettes in the North Pacific. He was also grievously wounded in combat, lost many a close friend and colleague and thus resolved to say farewell to pulp fiction and devote himself to what it had supported these many years—namely, his serious research.

But in no way was the LRH literary saga at an end, for as he wrote some thirty years later, in 1980:

"Recently there came a period when I had little to do. This was novel in a life so crammed with busy years, and I decided to amuse myself by writing a novel that was pure science fiction."

That work was *Battlefield Earth: A Saga of the Year 3000*. It was an immediate *New York Times* bestseller and, in fact, the first international science fiction blockbuster in decades. It was not, however, L. Ron Hubbard's magnum opus, as that distinction is generally reserved for his next and final work: The 1.2 million word *Mission Earth*.

> **Final Blackout**
> *is as perfect a piece of science fiction as has ever been written.*
>
> —**Robert Heinlein**

How he managed those 1.2 million words in just over twelve months is yet another piece of the L. Ron Hubbard legend. But the fact remains, he did indeed author a ten-volume *dekalogy* that lives in publishing history for the fact that each and every volume of the series was also a *New York Times* bestseller.

Moreover, as subsequent generations discovered L. Ron Hubbard through republished works and novelizations of his screenplays, the mere fact of his name on a cover signaled an international bestseller. . . . Until, to date, sales of his works exceed hundreds of millions, and he otherwise remains among the most enduring and widely read authors in literary history. Although as a final word on the tales of L. Ron Hubbard, perhaps it's enough to simply reiterate what editors told readers in the glory days of American Pulp Fiction:

He writes the way he does, brothers, because he's been there, seen it and done it!

THE STORIES FROM THE GOLDEN AGE

Your ticket to adventure starts here with the Stories from the Golden Age collection by master storyteller L. Ron Hubbard. These gripping tales are set in a kaleidoscope of exotic locales and brim with fascinating characters, including some of the most vile villains, dangerous dames and brazen heroes you'll ever get to meet.

The entire collection of over one hundred and fifty stories is being released in a series of eighty books and audiobooks. For an up-to-date listing of available titles, go to www.goldenagestories.com.

AIR ADVENTURE

141

FAR-FLUNG ADVENTURE

SEA ADVENTURE

TALES FROM THE ORIENT

MYSTERY

FANTASY

SCIENCE FICTION

WESTERN

Battle the Thirst for Revenge in the Town of Superstition!

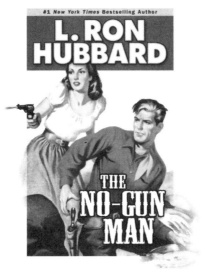

As a young man Monte Calhoun thought the measure of a man was how hard he could drink and how straight he can shoot. But, as principled as a young Jimmy Stewart, several years back East have changed him. He has become *The No-Gun Man*. Monte's civilized now... even if that means refusing to avenge the murder of his own father. But in a land of outlaws and ambushes, it's only a question of how far Monte will be pushed before he pushes back ... with a vengeance.

Blaze a bloody trail back to the American frontier as the audio version of *The No-Gun Man* shows how wild the Wild West can make a man.

Get
The No-Gun Man

JOIN THE PULP REVIVAL
America in the 1930s and 40s

Pulp fiction was in its heyday and 30 million readers were regularly riveted by the larger-than-life tales of master storyteller L. Ron Hubbard. For this was pulp fiction's golden age, when the writing was raw and every page packed a walloping punch.

That magic can now be yours. An evocative world of nefarious villains, exotic intrigues, courageous heroes and heroines—a world that today's cinema has barely tapped for tales of adventure and swashbucklers.

Enroll today in the Stories from the Golden Age Club and begin receiving your monthly feature edition selected from more than 150 stories in the collection.

You may choose to enjoy them as either a paperback or audiobook for the special membership price of $9.95 each month along with FREE shipping and handling.